ROMANCE SPIES COLLECTION VOLUME 2

CONNOR WHITELEY

No part of this book may be reproduced in any form or by any electronic or mechanical means. Including information storage, and retrieval systems, without written permission from the author except for the use of brief quotations in a book review.

This book is NOT legal, professional, medical, financial or any type of official advice.

Any questions about the book, rights licensing, or to contact the author, please email connorwhiteley@connorwhiteley.net

Copyright © 2023 CONNOR WHITELEY

All rights reserved.

DEDICATION
Thank you to all my readers without you I couldn't do what I love.

AUTHOR OF THE BETTIE ENGLISH PRIVATE
EYE MYSTERIES

CONNOR WHITELEY

DROP AT
THE BAR

A GAY SPY ROMANTIC SUSPENSE SHORT STORY

DROP AT THE BAR
22nd October 2022
Brighton, England

Arthur Jeffo might have been 24 years old and he might have once really, really loved the gayness, clubs and men of Brighton but for some reason he didn't really feel like he could enjoy it tonight.

Arthur stood next to a large fake wooden bar that was thankfully clean without a single drop of sticky alcohol on it, which was surprising considering how bad the rest of the bar or club looked.

The floors of the bar were smooth, white with a few black marks on them from shoes and boots and whatever else the clientele had decided to wear, and to be honest Arthur would have been very surprised if fighting in this bar was an alien concept to them.

All around the bar there were very tasteful and attractive square wooden tables of different heights to size the taller and shorter guests, and it really did help to add a little texture to the entire bar and even some depth. Arthur just smiled to himself as that was his interior designer training kicking in, something after a breakup with an awful boyfriend he had wanted to largely forget.

Clearly that wasn't happening.

The beautiful smell of hot sexy men's earthy, fruity and very manly aftershave filled the bar as Arthur subtly (and failed at that) watched the young hot men walking about in all their different sexualities, sex appeal and heights.

There was a group of guys in the far corner next to a dark staircase that Arthur really didn't want to know what it led down to, and those men were all wearing tight black leather pants that really highlighted how hot they were with cowboy hats, checked shirts and even cowboy boots.

It was clear they were part of a stag do or something and they were really hot, and maybe if Arthur wasn't strictly here on business then he might have been tempted to have a go at one of the men.

They were definitely hot enough.

But he was here on business, working for a top national newspaper and he was meant to be meeting a source, a corporate spy, that was meant to be bringing him top secret files on how the company was abusing its staff. This was exactly the sort of information that Arthur had been dying to get his hands on so he could make a name for himself and prove himself worthy for a promotion or two.

And then hopefully, and Arthur was seriously

hoping, then he might be able to breathe and actually slow down a fraction in his crazy life so he might be able to meet a man again.

He would love that.

"What's your poison sugar?" a young woman asked from behind the bar.

Arthur just smiled at her for a moment, she was good-looking with her smooth facial features, dark chocolate eyes and her long wavy brown hair. Arthur wouldn't have been surprised if she had gotten a lot of male attention here but then he realised that a large group of men were staring at her and trying to call her over.

"Oh I don't know," Arthur said. "It might take me a while to decide,"

Arthur was glad to see the young woman smile at him, at least he was right about the young woman wanting to get away from the large group of men.

The sound of the loud almost-deafening music (and Arthur seriously couldn't tell what music it was meant to be), people shouting at each other and Arthur could have sworn there were fights breaking out in the far corners of the bar, this definitely wasn't Arthur's sort of scene, he much preferred places were he could sit down, talk to a cute boy and actually be able to hear them properly.

This really wasn't that sort of place.

But he was here on business, he had to secure the information to get a job promotion and if needed he needed to make sure the corporate spy he was meeting was safe.

Arthur never ever wanted someone to get hurt for trying to do the right thing.

Arthur had never met a spy at all before so he didn't have a clue about what to expect, but if this company was onto the spy then Arthur wanted to protect them, because this spy was trying to improve the lives of their fellow workers and that was something that Arthur seriously admired.

But he just didn't have a clue what he was walking into.

Not a clue at all.

***

Professional Corporate Spy Noah Davis felt like such an amateur fool as he walked the narrow cobblestone streets of Brighton with its ancient bars and clubs forced into walls and spaces that he was surprised they actually fitted in. The bright lights and massive crowds of men and women and underage people were right in his face and this wasn't a controlled environment in the slightest.

The damn bar that Noah was meant to be meeting this reporter in might have been close but it was a mistake to choose somewhere in Brighton.

The cold crisp night was chilling Noah's skin down to the bone which wasn't a bad thing as it kept him alert and focused and ready to act, but this wasn't ideal.

Noah slowly walked through the cobblestone street, gliding through hot drunk men in their tight jeans and shirts and breathing in their sensational aftershave that made him really horny. It had been ages since Noah had been with a man, he had been too busy for the past two years going into companies, exposing their secrets and getting paid hundreds of thousands of pounds for doing it. It wasn't an easy job, but it was fun, exciting and Noah really felt like he was making a difference by doing it.

Yet Noah would have preferred to meet away from Brighton, the home city of the company he had been investigating, and the major problem was that too many of the higher-ups in the company partied on Saturday nights in this area.

If they saw him, which he just knew they would, then Noah could be exposed and blacklisted from the industry as a spy and never work in a corrupt company again. That was a massive risk and it was all because he had heard of some hot reporter.

It was stupid really that Noah had been reading a newspaper of all things (he was never going to let his phone die again) and he had been reading a great article written by an Arthur Jeffo and there was a cute little picture of him at the bottom of the article. A sensible person might have taken that as a sign that Noah wanted to do a man sooner and actually needed to get back out on the dating scene.

But nope.

Noah took it as a sign that he needed to meet up with this hottie, risk his entire career and he didn't even know if this Arthur person was gay or that way inclined. It was a hell of a lot to risk for no reason.

Noah just smiled to himself as he felt his body turn warm and excited and his stomach relaxed because it was this thrill that he lived for and this was exactly why he kept doing his spying job because it was dangerous and extremely fun.

After walking down the street a little more and gliding past some very drunk women, Noah hooked a left and went towards a little bar that looked like a tavern from Victorian times.

He went through the wooden door, nodded politely to the bouncer that really didn't look like he gave a toss about Noah's age and he went inside.

The bar was definitely too loud and ugly and chaotic for Noah's liking. There were at least three fighting at the far end of the bar but thankfully the bar that served drinks weren't in that direction and in all fairness there were plenty of hot men in the bar too.

Noah started to make his way through the surprisingly clean wooden floors over towards the bar when he just stopped.

Standing right next to the bar was possibly the most beautiful man he had ever seen. He instantly recognised it as Arthur Jeffo and bloody hell that little stupid photo didn't do him justice at all.

Arthur was a fucking hot man with a typical gym body, manly sexy broad shoulders and a very thin waist that Noah couldn't wait to wrap his arms around, and Noah just knew that Arthur had a solid stomach without a shred of fat on it.

And even Arthur's face was divine with his strong manly jawline, amazing smile as he spoke to the young woman behind the bar and his short brown hair was so perfect that Noah was rather pleased that his wayward parts were flaring to life and tenting.

His heart was beating faster and his head was going light and Noah wanted to talk with Arthur right now.

"Noah?" an elderly man said.

Noah turned around and just gave the elderly man a fake smile when he saw that his boss was standing only a few metres from him.

This wasn't going to end well at all.

***

"Have a good night," Arthur said to the pretty young woman behind the bar as she went off to deal with other customers.

Arthur had really liked talking to her and she was actually rather interesting with her only working in the bar because she needed the money to start her own beauty business that was already starting to seriously take off.

And with more and more coming into the bar now, the temperature was starting to increase, but not too much as the room was still comfortable.

Arthur looked away from the wonderful bar and the young woman and really focused on the incoming crowd. He noticed a lot of hot beautiful men come in and out of the bar with their friends with a good night of clubbing and partying and probably some more adult activity ahead.

But there was one guy that seriously caught his attention.

In amongst the sea of other hot men coming into the bar, there was a young cute man that made Arthur's face light up, his smile reached ear to ear and Arthur felt like the entire world had stopped.

The young man was extremely cute with his dark brown buzzcut, his smooth expensive white shirt and black jeans that made him look smart and even more beautiful without making him seem like a poser.

He was so beautiful and Arthur felt his throat dry up and for the first time in his entire life, Arthur honestly didn't know what to say, do or even write in his article. His mind was starting to go blank for a moment until he noticed an elderly man start talking to the cute man.

Arthur felt like that wasn't good.

For a moment Arthur was concerned that he was just being jealous and almost overprotective of the cute man, he had sadly felt that feeling before, and this one just felt different.

Arthur was feeling an instinct that he had honed in recent years from meeting with informants, the odd (amateur) corporate spy and other confidential sources. This was the type of feeling that Arthur only felt when he knew there was danger.

Arthur needed to get to that cute man, get the information and go.

Arthur quickly ordered a drink of cola and pretended to walk over to the cute man acting completely drunk.

"You shouldn't be here. We know what you're up to," the elderly man said to the cute man.

Arthur's stomach immediately tensed but he kept acting drunk and walking over to the cute man. If this elderly man did truly suspect the cute man as a spy then this could get very ugly very quickly.

"We know you're gay and you will never get a promotion in our company," the elderly man said.

Arthur felt totally relieved when the elderly man said that and he was so close to the cute man that hopefully he could save him sooner rather than later. But the only problem with acting drunk was that Arthur sadly couldn't move as quick as he wanted.

"And what do you know about spies and missing files in the company?" the elderly man asked.

Arthur pretended to trip over and fell upon the cute man. Arthur really loved feeling the cute man's hot, hard and slightly sweaty body as he acted to recover whilst drunk.

"Play along," Arthur whispered to the cute man as he breathed in his hot manly scent that was really exciting Arthur.

The cute man wrapped his arms around Arthur like he was helping a stupid drunk, said bye to the elderly man and pretended to help Arthur over to a bar stool in a dark corner on the opposite side of the bar.

"Nicely played," Arthur said as he sat on a very uncomfortable and very worn bar stool and pressed his back against the warm wall.

"You don't get to be as good of a spy as me without learning a few things. The corporate spy game is deadly, messy and very dangerous at times," the cute man said.

Arthur just focused on every single sexy little word that came out of the man's big beautiful lips.

"The name's Noah and it's good to meet you at last Arthur," the cute man said.

Arthur was so glad to finally have this cute man's name but it was a little weird that Noah knew his.

"Relax Arthur," Noah said. "I always research the peeps I'm meeting. It keeps me alive so I wanted to be sure I was safe and giving the info to a good journalist,"

Arthur instantly knew what Noah meant. He had met plenty of journalists that would happily give the corrupt information back to the corporation the spy or whistle-blower stole it from, for the right price of course.

Arthur wasn't one of those journalists. The people had a right to know what corruption and laws were being broken by these massive monster companies.

And Arthur had to admit it was really hot to meet someone so beautiful but also so knowledgeable about companies, journalism and how everything worked behind the scenes.

"Do you have the info?" Arthur asked.

Arthur loved seeing Noah mockingly smile at him.

"You're all business aren't you?" Noah asked. "And anyway look at your nine o'clock with the elderly man,"

Arthur subtly looked over and saw the elderly man that was presumably from the company beautiful Noah was trying to expose and he was watching them with a large group of other people.

There had to be at least ten men watching Arthur and Noah and that really unnerved him. This wasn't good in the slightest.

"They know I stole the information and files and I wasn't as careful as I normally am," Noah said. "They're watching us to see when I made a mistake, they're exposed us and we'll probably get arrested for stealing information or corporate espionage,"

As farfetched as some of that sounded Arthur was all too familiar with some of the lies that big companies told to discredit journalists and articles that attacked them.

"Then we need to exchange the information and get out of the bar and disappear without getting caught," Arthur said with a massive smile on his face.

This was going to be great fun.

Noah smiled too and Arthur was really struggling to focus on anything else but this beautiful sexy man in front of him.

"Care for a dance cutie?" Arthur asked gesturing

Noah to take his hand.

As soon as Noah took Arthur's hand, Arthur loved how soft, sexy and smooth Noah's wonderful hands were. And that was all before Arthur realised how amazing it felt to hold Noah and the sheer attraction and passion he felt for this beautiful man was almost overwhelming.

Arthur liked Noah a damn sight more than he ever wanted to admit. Even to himself.

***

As stunning Arthur pulled Noah onto the dance floor which was a very fancy term for a tableless section of the bar that allowed people to dance on the hard wooden floors, Noah was so amazed how horny he was and how much he just wanted Arthur in that moment.

Arthur wasn't only the hottest man he had ever seen but he was also smart, intelligent and very, very crafty.

Noah just hoped that their plan of exchanging the information, getting out of the club and disappearing into the night would work.

It was even harder with Noah's bosses and other people that he suspected were cops watching their every move. Noah was going to have to be very careful and very clever and he had to protect the hot stunning man that was dancing with him.

Noah was rather grateful that the current song playing had a very sexual and sensual rhythm to it and whilst the vast majority of the bar were focused on them. His bosses and the undercover cops really didn't want to watch two men dance against each other.

The great sound of people cheering, singing along and more gay and straight couples joining the dance floor echoed off the bright walls of the bar.

The wonderful smell of hot sweaty men and women and aftershave and alcohol filled the dance floor and as soon as a group of straight people obscured the view from the undercover cops Noah got to work.

"Show time," Noah whispered into Arthur's ear.

Noah carefully and subtly took the USB stick with the information out of his pocket and started moving his hand all over Arthur's amazing body.

Noah feeling up Arthur's wonderful chest, hard stomach and lower regions definitely wasn't needed for the mission but it was fun.

And it certainly made Noah know for certain that Arthur was very gay, aroused and into him. Exactly how Noah liked his jobs.

The straight couples moved away and Noah noticed that the elderly man and the group of cops had moved.

They were gone.

"Excuse me," a young man said.

Noah pretended to trip forward and grab Arthur's very firm ass. Slipping the USB stick into his back pocket in the process.

Then Noah broke away, wrapped his arms round

Arthur's shoulders and smiled at the rather cute male cop that was standing there showing them his police badge.

"Can we help you officer?" Arthur asked, like he was scared but of course Noah just knew that he was far from that.

"Sir can you please show me your hands," the cop said to Noah.

Noah nodded and showed the cop his hands but of course they were empty.

"Sir I believe you are in the procession of stolen property including highly confidential files that would inhibit and damage national security," the cop said.

Noah really forced himself not to smile, he had to give it to his bosses at the corrupt and abusive company. They certainly knew what lies and fake evidence to show the police.

"Oh my god," Arthur said taking a few steps back and sounding really high-pitched.

Noah loved it how Arthur was going to play the dumb-stupid-gay card.

"You mean he's a criminal. Oh my, I couldn't have that. I knew I shouldn't have come to a straight bar," Arthur said.

Noah forced himself not to laugh.

The cop smiled at Arthur. "It's okay sir. I just need to ask Noah a few questions but you're free to go. Have a good night,"

Arthur weakly smiled at the cop and started to back away.

Noah was so glad that Arthur was going to be able to slip away from the bar without suspicion with the information needed to expose the company.

As Arthur started to walk away Noah had to admit he looked stunning from the rear and Noah's horniest was seriously struggling to stay in check.

"Wait officer," the elderly man said. "He was acting drunk earlier and now he's fine. Something is dodgy with him too,"

Noah just frowned as his idiot bosses in their dark black suits surrounded Arthur and the cop too didn't look impressed.

Maybe their getaway wouldn't be as easy as he thought.

Noah just feared things were going to get very ugly for both of them.

And he had no clue how to save the cute stunning man he was really attracted to.

Not a clue at all.

***

Arthur was seriously starting to hate this absolutely stupid and pathetic and homophobic dick of an elderly man and the other men surrounding him on the dance floor. All Arthur wanted to do was expose a corrupt and abusive company but clearly there was no way that was going to happen for a little while.

Arthur had to escape from this mess.

"Sir," the male cop said, "I'll ask you once and then you're on your own. Do you have the stolen information on you?"

Arthur partly wanted to keep playing up the dumb-gay routine because it was so easy and it was the only thing working for him at the moment and sadly he just knew it was the only thing saving him for now.

Arthur looked over the wooden bar with the pretty young woman currently pouring a tray of drinks and she was watching him intensely.

He winked at her and she lowered her head and kept pouring the drinks.

Arthur doubted she was going to be worth any help but he had to try.

"Sir," the cop said.

"Listen mate," Arthur said in a very high pitched voice. "I ain't a criminal, I ain't even from Brighton I came here fun. I didn't know it was so criminal honest,"

"He's lying," the elderly man said.

The cop looked at the ground and then exchanged glances with Noah and Arthur. Arthur really loved how cool and collective and confident Noah looked given the situation.

Even now with them both about to be arrested Noah still looked so hot and beautiful.

The cop took out his handcuffs. "Both of you are coming with me. We can sort this out down at the station,"

Arthur took a few steps back as the cop came towards him. Why the cop was going to arrest him first he didn't know.

"Wait officer. I'm innocent. Please, believe me," Arthur said.

The young woman walked past holding a massive tray of shots and Arthur instantly took out the USB stick.

The young woman tripped and the entire tray of drinks went over the cop.

The woman fell to the floor but Arthur subtly passed her the USB stick.

Arthur saw her quickly stuff the stick in her bra.

"I'm so sorry officer," the young woman said.

"It's okay Miss. It was an accident," the officer said with a massive schoolboy smile.

"She's lying," the elderly man said. "She-"

"Silence," the cop said and he just looked at Arthur.

"Officer," Arthur said. "Pat me down right here and now and you'll see I have nothing to hide,"

The cop didn't seem convinced but with the spilt alcohol dripping off him he clearly wanted to go back to the station and get changed and probably just go home so he nodded.

Arthur parted his legs and held his legs sideways and the cop quickly patted him down. Arthur hated the rough feeling of the cop's touch-up but the cop was done.

The cop even remembered to search all of Arthur's pockets which a lot of cops forget but of course there was nothing to find.

"You're free to go and-" the officer said before he realised that Noah was gone.

"Officer-" the elderly man said.

The cop shot the elderly man and the rest of his large group a warning finger and just stormed off. Clearly the cop was done with the elderly man's stupid games and he left the bar.

The young woman walked past Arthur again and she subtly slipped the USB stick into the back of his jeans. Arthur had to admit she was flat out amazing and he was going to pay her later for all of her wonderful help.

Arthur just walked out of the bar but now he was really curious about where in the world that hot beautiful man Noah had gone to.

And why had he left so quickly without even saying goodbye?

***

As bad as Noah felt for just abandoning sexy Arthur in the bar, it was needed and from years of experience that was the only way to confuse and make the cop angry enough to just leave the two of them alone.

Noah sat on Brighton beach in the darkness with the pitch black sea in front of him crashing into the cold sand. The coldness radiated up through his jeans but Noah didn't really mind too much, it was the chills had made him feel alive and okay and alert.

In the darkness of the sandy beach seemed to stretch on endlessly to his sides with the bright almost-fun-fair lights in the distance and the lights from the hotels and casinos on the seafront burning away some of the darkness.

But after the mission, Noah just really enjoyed the quiet sound of the crashing waves, the coldness of the sand and the lack of people. But Noah still couldn't believe he had actually left that stunning man in the bar.

It was so normal for Noah to leave people behind and just get out of situations with cops, companies and everything else that he had actually done it without thinking, but Arthur was different.

And it was that feeling that Arthur was special that annoyed him, in a good way.

Normally Noah loved being with so many men, having great sex with him and then leaving the relationship after a few weeks (or days more often than not) it was just easier with his corporate spy lifestyle. But after meeting someone as stunning, clever and cunning as Arthur, Noah wasn't sure if he wanted that life anymore.

Ever since Noah had been a little boy he had dreamed of coming home to a stunning man after a mission, kissing him and just talking about it, like his parents did. Noah's parents worked hard every single day of their life, came home and told each other everything. They were both so loving and caring to each other.

Noah just wanted to do that with a man.

As much as Noah didn't want to admit it, he was

going to have to risk everything again by going back to that bar, showing his face and making sure that Arthur was okay.

And if there was a choice between Arthur getting arrested and charged with the corporate espionage instead of him, Noah was perfectly okay with changing places for the first time ever. Not that this had ever happened before anyway.

Noah stood up and started to walk towards the concrete stairs upwards to the seafront when he just stopped and smiled when he saw stunning Arthur was walking down towards him.

And he wouldn't have blamed Arthur for leaving him, hating him or even exposing his corporate spying activities for almost getting him arrested, but Arthur honestly did look happy to see him.

It was in that moment that Noah knew that if Arthur wanted a relationship then there was a great chance that everything was going to be okay, wonderful and even magical.

And there wasn't a single man Noah would rather spend his time with. Arthur was wonderfully stunning, clever and cunning and that was exactly the sort of man Noah wanted.

He just hoped that Arthur felt the exact same way.

***

A month later, Arthur was sitting up on his massive Queen-size bed looking at his tablet early on a Sunday morning reading the news headlines when he learnt that his article had caused shockwaves throughout the UK.

Arthur pulled the very beautiful and sexy and seriously hot Noah closer to him as he slept in only his tight black boxers that thankfully left very little to the imagination. The bright morning sunlight shone through Arthur's large windows and the bright blue walls of his bedroom amplified the sunlight to make the bedroom feel even more perfect and spacious and airy.

Some other interior designer tricks that he had learnt from that damn ex-boyfriend.

Arthur really loved how his article had exposed the entire string of abusive, corrupt and illegal practices that not only Noah's company used but a ton of other companies in the same industry. Arthur's article had even become so major that it had made international news and Arthur had received ten job offers from all over the world.

Arthur would be lying if he wasn't considering travelling to New Zealand, Canada or mainland Europe to tackle some corrupt companies in these countries.

But as Noah woke up and kissed him, Arthur just savoured the passionate, soft kisses that he had really loved waking up to every single morning for the past month. He had even helped Noah on another corporate espionage case that was surprisingly tense, and that had only made him love Noah even more.

And then it dawned on Arthur that for the first

time in maybe ever, he actually realised that there was more to life than work, news stories and promotions.

There was also love in life, and as he slowly ran his fingers down Noah's hard chest and stomach, and loved the feeling of attraction that pulsed through him, Arthur honestly realised that love was the most important part of life after all.

And as Noah took Arthur's tablet away and started kissing him and got on top of him, Arthur just knew that they were made for each other. They both loved their work, they both loved exposing corrupt companies and most importantly they both seriously loved each other.

Those were the three most important things to Arthur and he was seriously looking forward to spending a lot of time with Noah and definitely growing old with him.

Because this really was true love.

LOVING TO SPY

Part-time Intelligence Officer Steven Page really loved working in the secret computer labs at Kent University. He really enjoyed the labs' smooth white walls filled with anti-scanning technology, perfectly soft blue carpet and all the little computer booths that shot out from the main area he was sitting in so other officers could work.

Thankfully, it was only him working the labs today so far, and in all honesty he wasn't really sure why it was called a computer lab considering the only computers in the room were in the little booths that shot out from the main area. And even then, all the computer booths were shut behind monitored wooden doors.

But Steven didn't really mind the strange detail, he just loved the location because it was quiet, peaceful and he could actually crack on with all his university assignments, readings and Intelligence work without anyone watching him.

Steven sat at a large round wooden table that leant to one side because of a dodgy leg that no one had cared to fix just yet, and Steven wasn't too bothered either. He had dealt with a lot more trouble than a simple wobbly table leg.

The wonderful aromas of fruity blackberry tea, strawberry pastries and rich creamy hot chocolate filled the air from Steven's breakfast that he had bought in with him, but at the moment he was a little too busy looking at his black high-security laptop going through the various morning emails he had been sent.

Steven seriously loved having parents that were some of the UK's best Intelligence Officers, and he loved that he got to work with them from time to time with other students at the university, but he had never known how many emails he would have to deal with.

Most of the emails were great. Like new assignments, new threats to the university (because it handled a lot of top-secret government research that China, Russia and Iran were very interested in) and there were even some well-done emails from heads of departments congratulating Steven and his friends on their work.

But some of the emails were a lot less interesting.

Officially, Steven was a political psychology student at the university so it didn't sound strange for him to talk to his friends with an in-depth knowledge about how the political worlds worked around the world, but some emails from the British secret service (MI6) made it sound like impossible terrorist threats were headed to the university.

Of course, it was just MI6 being overdramatic because they weren't meant to be operating on UK soil, but they still made Steven's stomach tighten each time he read them.

The sound of students laughing, talking and discussing their latest assignments outside made Steven just smile for a few moments, because he honestly couldn't imagine not knowing what he knew about the world, the university and the threats he faced.

He loved the work, it was amazing and he got to work with his amazing friends that were meant to be showing up later, but he was still a young man at the end of the day. And it had been so long since he had hooked up, spoken to or even smiled at a cute man.

Steven was in his final year at university and he had only had one hook-up with a sexy guy in those three years, that wasn't a good sex life by any definition, and now Steven was finding that he was having to lie more and more with his non-intelligence friends about his non-existent sex life.

It was even worst that Kent University had a thriving gay scene, but Steven had never actually gone to any gay events to meet people, and with the months ticking down until he left for good. He was definitely starting to doubt he was ever going to find some fun, action or maybe even a boyfriend whilst he was still a student.

Steven's laptop pinged and Steven smiled at the email from his amazing mum that was addressed to him, his best friend Natasha and another straight man in their friendship group. There were a lot of files attached but the email mentioned something about Iran preparing to do a massive cyberattack against the university at any moment.

Steven instantly knew exactly what the Iranians were after, it was so typical that as much as MI6, Counterterrorism and the entire UK intelligence community tried to hide the fact Kent University was conducting nuclear research for the government, the UK's bloody enemies always found out.

Steven had been stationed and studying at Kent University for years and he still refused to believe the government's logic for conducting nuclear research at a university. Apparently, the UK's enemies were less likely to target a university compared to a government-owned site.

Steven didn't believe that for a second.

But there was one line of his mother's email that really caught Steven's eye, *Find out how the attack will be launched*.

Steven was almost an expert in Iran, geopolitics and intelligence work. But he knew next to nothing about the inter-workings of cyberattacks.

Not a single clue.

And with a major cyberattack happening any time now Steven was growing more and more concerned by the second.

***

University Student Phill Lee leant against the wonderfully warm red brick wall of his best friend Tom's accommodation block at their university. The day was perfectly warm for an autumn day without it being too cold, too warm and there was even the subtle dampness that made him just know it was autumn.

Phill had always loved the amazing season of autumn. It was nowhere near as awful and cold as winter, nor was it was as boiling and unbearable as summer, or a weird combination of winter and summer like spring. Autumn was a perfect standalone season that was perfect for Phill.

Phill wrapped his hands round the piping hot takeaway cup of coffee that was steaming and he was holding onto the cup like his life depended on it. That was the weird thing about the cold, it was only his hands that tended to feel cold or icy.

The rest of him was fine.

Phill waited for Tom to come out of the large glass doors next to him, but in the meantime, Phill focused on the amazing calmness of the early morning outside the accommodation block.

The large miniature lake that had a few ducks bobbing along twenty metres away was a great natural feature in amongst the concrete university campus that led onto a massive green field covered in white frost sloping down towards the city centre a few miles away.

Phill had always loved Canterbury, it was still a city but it didn't have the crazy feel of London or Manchester or Leeds.

And this early in the morning, the area around Tom's accommodation block was almost perfectly empty with no one walking along the narrow concrete paths that zig-zagged in-between all the different accommodation blocks.

Phill watched a cute young gay couple that he only knew were gay because the two fit men (clearly first years) were holding their gloved hands together, as they smiled and walked towards Canterbury City Centre. That was going to be a bit of a hike for them but Phill was really happy for them.

That was exactly what he wanted.

As bad as it sounded (and Phill couldn't believe it), he had been at university for four years now studying advance computer science with a year's work experience doing research at the university, and he hadn't dated a single man.

He had always been gay, his family had been the ones pushing him to find love and get a boyfriend, but Phill had just found himself too busy to get a boyfriend at university. Phill had dated a little during 6th form and at secondary school but he was a kid back then, he didn't know anything about relationships.

All Phill wanted now though was to have a real love at a relationship, sex and maybe love.

It was just annoying that Tom was straight, then all of Phill's problems would be solved and that was the standing joke between him and Tom.

But Phill still couldn't understand why in the world Tom had wanted to meet up with him early. They were already going into the city later tonight with some of their other friends to go clubbing, drinking and dancing.

Yet apparently Tom just had to see Phill this morning, it was so important that Phill couldn't miss it.

"Hi," Tom said as he walked out of his accommodation block.

Phill always just smiled at his best friend for a few moments whenever he first saw him. Phill really liked how great Tom looked in his black jeans, denim jacket and black designer trainers that made him look so cool and hot.

It was just such a shame he was so straight, and actually had a girlfriend.

Tom gestured they should start walking down the narrow concrete path that led towards the main campus, and Phill followed.

"Why you wanna see me?" Phill asked.

Tom grinned. "I can't tell you, but you will not be sorry you met up with me,"

Phill wanted to say something a little pathetic like he was already glad he called because he got to see him this morning. Damn it, Phill seriously needed to get with a man a lot sooner rather than later. He hated being this desperate.

"Okay," Phill said. "But why all the secrecy? Why don't you just tell me where we're going?"

Tom shrugged as he led them through a little concrete tunnel that went through an accommodation block towards the main campus. It was a great shortcut but Phill would never go through it in the dark, he wasn't that brave.

Phill was a little surprised when they came out of the tunnel and Tom hooked a right. No one ever went that way because the main campus was straight ahead.

Phill didn't argue, he only kept following Tom as they went down another narrow little pathway with bright orange leaf-covered trees to their left and grey concrete to their right.

After a few moments Tom went into a dark brown wooden building that Phill knew was the computer labs used by the Social Science Division and Phill just couldn't understand why Tom was taking him in there.

Phill didn't know a single person that actually used that building. It was often the butt of a joke because the computer labs looked like a massive shed-like building from the outside because it was completely made of wood.

"Come on please," Tom said, grinning. "You will definitely love this,"

As much as Phill didn't want to go in and he sort of felt like he was making a big mistake, he knew that

Tom was a great friend and he wouldn't make him do anything bad.

Phill went over to the computer labs, went through the large glass door and went into a room that he could only describe as a main area of sorts with its bright white walls, horrible blue carpet and tons of wooden doors that were presuming computer pods or something lining the walls.

"Who's that Tom?" a woman asked.

Phill looked at the group of people sitting at the end of the main area with their laptops resting on a round wooden table, but there was only one thing he could focus on.

Phill had absolutely no idea who the hell was the hot sexy man was sitting at the table. But by God he was the hottest man Phill had ever seen.

The man was wearing a very smart almost-business-like dark green jumper that made him look so stylish, hot and seriously highlighted how fit he was. Phill wouldn't have been surprised in the man had V-cut abs or something.

And the man had the most adorable face ever, he had massive innocent looking eyes, a killer smile and a strong, very manly jawline that Phill was really falling for.

Phill just looked at Tom quickly and he quickly realised that next to this man, Tom really didn't look that impressive.

"Who is he Tom?" the woman asked again.

"This is the man who's going to help us," Tom

said.

And as much as a little voice in the back of his head was telling Phill to run and that he had walked into something very wrong. All he could do was focus on the sexy man with the smart dark green jumper.

He was seriously hot.

***

Steven had always known Tom was probably the smartest and most resourceful of their group of three, and Natasha had only showed up moments before Tom had turned up, but for Tom this seemed very, very strange.

For a spilt second, Steven had even thought that the new guy could be an enemy agent that had forced Tom to come here, but they had all been trained far too well for that to happen and Tom wasn't giving any of the twenty subtle signs that he was in danger.

With that possibility now thankfully dead, Steven allowed the black plastic and fabric chair he was sitting on to take his full weight, and he really focused on the new man.

It thankfully didn't take him too longer realise how amazingly hot and very cute this hottie was.

The man was seriously fit with his slim waist and the white t-shirt he was wearing definitely highlighted how fit he was, and if anything years of intelligence training definitely told Steven it was that the hottie worked out. Not a lot, but enough to keep himself fit and looking very, very nice.

Steven really loved the hottie's pointy face,

slightly brown beard and his blond crewcut that looked so smooth, attractive and alluring. It was taking every single gram of Steven's willpower not to go over to the hottie and run his fingers through that soft hair right there and then.

Then he realised the hottie was actually staring and smiling at him too.

Steven's stomach tensed. It tightened into a knot. Sweat poured off his forehead.

It had been ages since a man had liked him and focused on him. It wasn't natural and Steven had no idea what to do. Should he speak? Introduce himself? Offer the hottie a seat?

Steven stood up then realised his throat was too dry to speak and now everyone was staring at him.

"I…" was all Steven could manage.

"What do you mean this man is going to help us?" Natasha asked.

Steven forced himself to sit back down and focus on Natasha in her long brown hoodie (that was bound to be hiding a knife or two, or three), jeans and winter boots.

"Help you?" the hottie asked. "Why would you need my help?"

Steven had to admit that he needed to say something to get answers but his damn throat was still too dry.

"You have an assignment to do and we need the expertise of a computer science expert and HQ has cleared him," Tom said.

Natasha threw her arms up in the air and Steven completely agreed that Tom should not have mentioned HQ.

"They also wanted to recruit him," Tom said.

Now Tom had really crossed the point of no return and Steven gave a careful eye on Natasha in case she went for the hottie.

"What the hell is this?" the Hottie asked, clearly getting more and more concerned. "What the hell do you want to recruit me for?"

The only major problem with all of this, and Steven seriously hated this problem, was that their work at the university was extremely top-secret because not even the university itself knew that MI5 and MI6 and other agencies were running operations to keep the university's research out of enemy hands. And even if their operation was hinted at and even partially exposed then this would all end very, very badly.

All of their careers in intelligence work could be over way before they had even begun.

"Why the hell are you telling hottie this?" Steven asked, a little more forcefully than he meant to.

"Because the Iranians are here. There's an attack about to happen and we need expertise," Tom said.

Steven just looked at Natasha. "Well I guess we now have to brief the hottie,"

"You think I'm a *hottie*," he said.

Steven's mouth dropped instantly as he soon as he realised how silly he had been. Damn it, he was never this silly around a boy normally.

"Sit down," Natasha said to both Tom and the hottie.

Steven just stared at the hottie as he carefully walked over to their round wooden table and Steven was really fighting the urge to run his hand under the hottie's white t-shirt and kiss those amazing lips.

Steven wanted to laugh at himself for being so head-over-heels for this guy, but he forced himself to behave.

After a moment of hesitation the hottie sat down next to Steven, and Steven had to sit on his hands to make sure he didn't accidentally do anything.

"I know your name is Phill Lee," Natasha said, "and I know Tom wouldn't lie about HQ clearing you and wanting you to join us. We are a small unit working for the UK government on protecting the university's top-secret research against the UK's enemies,"

Steven had to admit Natasha was always great at giving the official talk about what they did and she did it with such a serious tone that Steven didn't know whether to be scared or not.

And Phill was a very hot name for a very hot man.

"Really?" Phill asked, laughing like this was all some kind of joke.

Natasha folded her arms.

"You guys don't work for the government," Phill said, laughing so hard no sound was coming out.

"It's true," Tom said.

Phill kept laughing and shook his head. Steven just smiled because he had seen this reaction plenty of times and it was always fun to watch, but not when they had a deadline and an attack to stop.

Against his better judgement, Steven took out a hand from under his butt and gently grabbed one of Phill's shoulders.

Steven was instantly amazed at how wonderful Phill's shoulders were. He definitely worked out and his shoulders felt amazingly toned.

Now Steven was just wondering what else was toned so perfectly. And Steven really enjoyed the sheer chemistry that was flowing between him and Phill.

"It's true," Steven said, amazed he could even force that out.

Then Phill stopped laughing, grinning and smiling. His face just went pale and he frowned.

"And," Steven said, "unless you help us figure out how to stop a cyberattack Iran is going to get their hands on a lot of nuclear research,"

Phill's face went even paler and Steven fully understood why.

This was bad. Very bad indeed.

***

Phill flat out couldn't believe this was actually happening. He couldn't understand in the slightest why the hell the government was spying on the university? And could these people really be trusted?

Phill didn't really know how he could possibly believe them. It just seemed so crazy that they were spies or whatever they called themselves, it was so strange because they looked so normal. Phill would have imagined them to look like older men in posh suits.

They definitely weren't wearing them as they all sat around the little round wooden table.

And the fact that they wanted him to join them or help them or just do something for them was even crazier.

"Time is ticking," the woman called Natasha said.

Phill slowly nodded his head. He didn't know what to do. This was all too much information, he had truly believed that he was going on a nice meet-up with his best friend. He didn't know he was about to enter the spy game.

Then Phill just focused on the really cute beautiful man sitting next to him. He had to admit the man had been acting strange ever since he saw him, but there was something so cute about him.

"We need to know how Iran could pull a cyberattack on the university," the cutie said. Phill was surprised, it was the most the cute man had said to him all day.

"Who are you?" Phill asked.

The cutie smiled. "Steven,"

"Boys. Men. Lovebirds," Natasha said. "Focus. Focus. Focus,"

Phill and Steven laughed and it was so great to feel their attraction to each other run through Phill. He really wanted to get to know Steven a lot better.

"Well," Phill said, deciding the best way to make Steven like him was to prove his intelligence, "Iran, if what you say is true, couldn't pull off a normal cyberattack by hacking into the computer systems from the outside. The university has security too good for that,"

Phill loved it how Steven was on the edge of his seat and hanging onto Phill's every word.

"At best Iran might be able to break the first few levels of defence into student records and stuff but they wouldn't be able to get to the research," Phill said.

Natasha nodded and looked at Tom.

"How would *you* commit the attack?" Steven asked grinning.

Phill loved Steven's sense of humour. It was a very well-kept secret that most of the time computer science students wanting to focus on security had to think just as much about how to break into computer systems as how to defend them.

"This is a university with a lot of deliveries. I would infect of the new pieces of equipment being delivered," Phill said.

"Oh," Tom said. "He's good. Can we keep him?"

Phill loved how wide Steven's grin got. He looked so cute and everyone looked at Natasha who he was starting to understand must have been their leader or something.

"Maybe," she said. "Tom look into what deliveries are scheduled to be made today. Focus on new equipment being delivered to the Georgian Building,"

Phill was impressed. He had always wondered why the Georgian building was basically off-limits to students and most staff members. He never would have guessed it was a top-secret research building.

"None," Tom said looking up from his laptop.

Steven clicked his fingers. "Actually I like Phill's idea but you're thinking about it wrong,"

Phill moved his chair over to be closer to this insanely hot man. Phill got so close to beautiful Steven that he could feel his body warmth radiating off him.

"There is a lot more equipment that goes into that building than deliveries," Steven said.

"What the researchers bring in themselves," Phill said. That was seriously clever of Steven to work out.

"But all researchers are checked weekly by MI5," Natasha said.

"Yes," Phill said, "but if what your saying is true. Then that only checks if they have turned against the government, not if they accidentally picked up something by mistake,"

"Oh God," Tom said.

"What?" Natasha asked.

"My stupid university," Steven said.

It took a few moments for Phill to realise what

Tom and beautiful Steven meant but they had all received tons of university emails about it.

Today was the only day staff members, postgraduate students and researchers were allowed to attend the Careers Fairs in the sports hall. There would be so many freebies and USB sticks being given away that it would only take one infected USB stick and one careless researcher for Iran's mission to be done.

Everyone stood up and packed their laptops away.

"How do we know what we're looking for?" Phill asked.

Everyone laughed.

"We won't until we get there," Steven said.

Everyone started heading out the door.

"Phill with me," Steven said as the others grabbed earpieces.

Phill's stomach filled with excitement at the idea of spending more time with wonderful Steven.

Even if they were about to hopefully stop a deadly cyberattack that would cost hundreds of thousands of lives if they failed.

***

Steven hated the massive sports hall that was the size of football pitches with hundreds of researchers, lecturers and other staff members tightly packed between rows upon rows of stalls.

It was a security nightmare and this was flat out not what Steven wanted at this moment.

But he was more than glad sexy Phill had joined him and Phill was so closely behind Steven that he could enjoy Phill's warmth against him.

Yet not quite as much as he wanted to because of the massive security threat looming over them as Steven glided through the crowd.

"What are we looking for?" Phill asked.

"Anything that isn't right," Steven said knowing exactly how vague that sounded to non-intelligence officers.

Steven seriously didn't like how many international governments and companies from the middle east were present today. Anyone of them could be an Iranian agent or none at all. Iran wouldn't be the first enemy of the UK to use its own people as agents.

This was a nightmare.

"No sign of anyone yet," Natasha said through Steven's earpiece.

This wasn't good. Steven felt completely lost in the sea of people that kept bumping and smashing into him.

Then he heard something.

Steven could have sworn he heard some Arabic but it was mutilated. Arabic normally sounded beautiful and rather lyrical in a strange fashion but the English accent in this Arabic murdered it.

Steven looked around but he couldn't see anything.

Phill carefully turned Steven around and looked

into his eyes. Steven really loved looking at Phill but this wasn't the time.

"What's wrong and think it through," Phill said.

Steven just nodded. He was too caught up in all of Phill's beauty but he was right, damn him. Steven needed to focus on the problem and not get overwhelmed in all the chaos this sports hall represented.

"We need to find possible Iranian agents in here. They want to give an infected USB stick to one of the nuclear researchers," Steven said.

"We need to go to the biggest physics research company here," Phill said.

Steven just nodded and glided through the crowd a lot more forcefully. He bumped into tons of men and women as he almost charged towards the government's stand here.

The UK government had a massive stand trying to show the researchers and lecturers how great and powerful it was. Steven knew it wasn't but it was always good to see the government try.

There were five middle-aged men standing behind the row of silver tables talking to researchers. Including one of the nuclear researchers from the university that Steven recognised.

The nuclear researcher with his balding head was talking to the only white man at the station and Steven just knew that he was the Iranian agent.

Steven charged through the crowd.

He watched the man give the researcher a USB

stick. They were talking in Arabic. The researcher was in on it.

"Stop!" Steven shouted.

The nuclear researcher legged it.

"We have a runner!" Steven shouted into his earpiece.

The white man whipped out a gun.

He fired.

People screamed.

Phill tackled Steven to the ground.

Steven rolled onto the ground.

Everyone ran to the exits.

He leapt up.

Charging across the sports hall.

Steven jumped into the air.

Leaping over the silver tables.

The white man fired again.

Missing Steven.

Two black men and an Asian woman tackled the gunman to the ground.

Steven landed next to the gunman.

Punching him in the face.

"You fool!" the white man shouted. "You have stopped nothing. My friends will end you and your pathetic country,"

Then the idiot started shouting and screaming in murdered Arabic and twisting the peaceful religion of Islam to their messed up ideology.

Steven just shook his head because their intel was very wrong here. This wasn't a plot sanctioned by the

Iranian government this was just a group of sad pathetic men wanting to do terror for no real reason at all except the silly ideas in their heads.

Three gunshots echoed.

Steven spun around.

A gunman fired at Steven.

Steven saw the muzzle flash.

The bullets screamed towards him.

Steven started to move.

Phill kicked Steven out the way.

Blood splashed against Steven's face.

Another shot went off.

Tom killed the gunman. Presumably the white man's only friend here.

Steven's eyes just widened as he looked at Phill. Phill was bleeding. Heavily.

"Call a fucking ambulance!" Steven shouted. His training kicking in.

Steven went straight over to Phill. Pressing down all his weight on the gunshot wounds.

Steven's hands were covered in blood but he just hoped he could stop the bleeding enough until help arrived.

And he seriously hoped it would arrive soon. Steven just couldn't lose beautiful Phill.

***

The next few hours were a complete and utter blur to Phill, the only thing he could possibly remember was the shouting of doctors in the operation theatre, them demanding more blood and the massive blinding light that shone in his face every single damn time he regained consciousness.

Phill didn't even really know where he was now. He of course knew that he was in a hospital of some sort because he was in a white plastic chair with more than enough medical equipment stuck into him, down his nose and constantly monitoring him, but he wasn't sure if he was still in Canterbury or not.

Phill managed to see the bright grey walls of the hospital room out of the corner of his eye, but Phill felt like he had been parked by the nurse or whoever had gotten him here, in front of a very beautiful view of a lustrous green field with sunflowers and wheat and blackberries gentle blowing in the wind through large floor-to-ceiling windows.

Of course Phill knew that this wasn't real and it was just an extremely effective TV screen, but it was beautiful.

And thankfully, the hospital didn't stink of horrible cleaning chemicals, death or anything else that Phill normally associated with hospitals. This one smelt very pleasant with hints of lavender, jasmine and orange that reminded him of Christmas pudding as a child with his family.

"I didn't think you were going to make it," Steven said behind him.

Phill felt his stomach churn and tighten for a moment.

He was only realising now that he was so relieved that Steven was well. When Phill had heard the gunshots and seen the man aim at Steven, Phill didn't know what came over him he just ran and had to make sure Steven wasn't hit.

It had never crossed his mind that he might be putting himself in danger or risk of injury or even risk of death. It just felt like the right thing to do and Phill honestly knew he wouldn't have changed it for anything.

He would always save Steven no matter what, which was weird in a way because Steven was a cute beautiful man that Phill had only met a few hours before.

But it was still true.

Steven walked into view and laughed at the TV screen in the windows in front of them both.

"These windows have gotten better since I was here last," Steven said folding his arms and looked at Phill.

Steven looked so cute in the same clothes as earlier, and for some reason Phill didn't know whether to be disturbed or not that Steven's hands were still covered in his blood.

Phill watched Steven get on his knees so his beautiful eyes were level with Phill's.

"Why did you save me?" Steven asked.

Phill laughed because it was such a weird question that Phill didn't see the point in. As his stomach tensed and flipped and filled with butterflies, the answer was so obvious because Steven was a beautiful man that was clever, kind and Phill could see how much he loved his job and helping people. It was those sort of people that just had to survive no matter what.

But Phill wanted to tell Steven a short answer.

"Because I like you and want you to live," Phill said, only now realising how true that was.

Steven laughed. "It isn't every day I get shot at and even have cute men trying to save me,"

"Tom's cute. Doesn't he save you?" Phill asked poking his tongue out at Steven.

"I prefer you to Tom," Steven said.

Phill smiled because it was amazing to see how much Steven's eyes were lighting up the more they talked, there was such a glimmer in his eyes that was so cute and Phill really wanted to get to know Steven a lot better.

"Just ask me out already," Phill said seductively.

Steven shrugged like this was nothing. "How do you know I'm into you. I am an intelligence officer, I could be playing you,"

Phill laughed and started coughing as his medical equipment bleeped. "I don't even know how long I have left. Do you really want a dying man to die not knowing if you like him or not?"

Steven playfully hit Phill and kissed him on the lips. Phill almost jumped out of his skin at the sheer electricity and passion that flowed between them. It was the most passionate and sensual kiss Phill had ever had.

"You aren't going to die," Steven said. "I won't

let that happen,"

And as Phill stared into Steven's perfect dark eyes, he just knew exactly what was going to happen now. They were going to keep talking, making each other laugh and almost certainly kiss a lot more for the rest of the day.

And beyond that, Phill had a very strong suspicion he had a boyfriend. A boyfriend that he would always protect, kiss and probably fall in love in a few weeks' time. Because Steven really was a perfect guy that was caring, clever and loving.

Exactly what he had always wanted in a man and now he was thankfully going to get it, and it had only taken him being shot to realise it.

***

After an amazing afternoon and evening with Phill, Steven just stood leaning against the perfectly warm wooden doorframe of Phill's hospital room as he watched Phill fall asleep. Phill looked so cute, peaceful and alive when he slept.

After the chaos and stress and worry of today and not knowing if wonderful Phill was ever going to make it, Steven just focused on Phill's fit sexy stomach rise and fall under the thin blue bedsheets that the hospital had provided him with. At least the little white plastic hospital bed was comfortable, but it would have been great if it had been bigger.

All Steven really wanted to do was spend the night with Phill just to make sure he was okay.

The quiet sound of nurses and doctors and

porters doing their rounds echoed up and down the bright grey corridors of the private hospital just south of canterbury that the UK Government had agreed to pay for, in exchange for Steven not going public with it was one of their people that was the danger today.

"Are you ever going to wash your hands?" Natasha and Tom asked as one as they kissed Steven's cheeks.

Steven looked down at his hands. All the blood had mostly gone away for the most part but they were still streaks from where he had tried (and thankfully had) saved Phill's life.

"The government and MI5 are grateful," Natasha said. "I caught the nuclear researcher with the memory stick before he could use it and it was their plan to use the careers fair as a cover so in case the stick was traced back to the researcher. He could say someone at the fair gave it to him,"

Steven nodded and forced himself to look away from beautiful Phill. "Thanks both, but Tom, why did you bring him today?"

Tom shrugged. "Because you need a boyfriend. Like seriously, when was the last time you had dick or something?"

Steven was so not going to dignify that with a response (mainly because he didn't know himself).

"Oh," Natasha said pulling out her phone. "I got an email just now and we all have a new assignment together and we have a new trainee with us who had accepted a job offer,"

Steven just grinned. He loved it that Phill had accepted the job offer he had been emailed about an hour ago.

"The three of us with Phill," Natasha said, "are heading to Sweden to go to university there as part of a joint operation with the Swedish Secret Service. Apparently, there's some neo-Nazi group trying to recruit British students,"

Steven felt his stomach buzz with excitement, all the tension in his shoulders and body relaxed and he was seriously looking forward to the future.

Because he was with his best friends in the entire world and now he was going to be with a very cute man that he could finally call his boyfriend, and after years of being an intelligence officer, Steven had very good senses about people and things and relationships.

And he just had a feeling that him and Phill weren't going to be breaking up for ages, if ever and he was perfectly fine, happy and delighted about that.

ROMANCE SPIES COLLECTION VOLUME 2

SPYING AROUND AN AUCTION
8th November 2022

Classified Location, Southern France

To MI6 Officer Scott Brody, there were exactly three things that classed a party as "too posh", "snobby" or "silly" for his liking, and with him being British he only knew all too well how stupid some English parties could be. For a party to be too much for Scott, it had to involve miniature food, formal suits and a live classical band that played such classical music that not even operas would dare to play it.

This event had all those three things perfectly.

Scott leant against the dark brown oak railing on the upper-level of a great chamber inside a very wonderful castle in the south of France. The floor Scott was standing on was a massive circle that didn't jet off into any rooms or serve any practical function, it was just an upper floor to allow guests to look down on the guests below them.

That was another definition of poshness or even

pompousness to Scott.

He really enjoyed the amazingly soft red carpet under his feet that was bouncy to walk on, the bright white walls with classical French paintings done by artists he had never heard of was pretty to look at and even French waiters walking round with champagnes flutes were very hot.

But Scott couldn't really focus on any of that, and he seriously wanted to focus on the hot French waiters because the French definitely knew how to produce gorgeous men. Instead Scott had to focus down on the floor below him.

To call it was a floor was a massive understatement because the chamber (that was probably a better word) was an immense red-carpeted dance floor where tons of hot French, Spanish and Chilian men were dancing with their wives as they both groped each other in their dresses and suits.

There was one particular Spanish man in the middle of the dance floor gently dancing with his wife wearing a particularly lovely dark blue suit that Scott really wouldn't have minded dancing with. He was so gorgeous.

Scott forced himself to look away as the classical band playing from their raised platform on the far side of the chamber got a little louder as they finished up their latest song, everyone clapped and the band immediately started into another song that Scott hadn't heard of before.

The entire castle smelt amazing with hints of

freshly roasted pork, frogs (that really did taste like chicken) and freshly poured champagne. It was a symphony of pleasure for the senses and Scott just knew he was going to enjoy this mission.

When MI6 had first asked him to come to southern France, he had to admit he was a little unsure because as much as he honestly loved the French (and their men) he wasn't sure if he was comfortable running an op on French soil. He normally worked in eastern Europe working against the Russians, Polish and criminal gangs.

Working so close to home was new for him.

As Scott focused on all the men and women walking about him on the upper floor and down in the chamber below, they all screamed money, power and corruption and this really was exactly where Scott loved to be.

There was meant to be an auction tonight for a number of illegal items, like slaves, US intelligence, top-secret codes and more, but Scott was only interested in one of the items.

Someone was selling information on where MI6's Most Wanted fugitive was located. That was the information he needed, and ever since he had learnt that, Scott hadn't been at all surprised when MI6 had said to forget about the rest as they tipped off the French Directorate-General for Internal Security so no doubt there would be a raid later on.

Scott hoped to be done by then.

MI6's Most Wanted fugitive was a woman by the

name of Sarah Mckinnon, a former MI6 officer turned international assassin responsible for assassinations on all 6 continents, killing entire squads of British troops in the Middle East and assassinating a Spanish Prime Minister only three months ago.

Sarah had to be found no matter what and Scott really wanted to kill her himself but that wasn't the mission just yet.

As the entire live band got even louder as they were about to finish their song, Scott was really looking forward to this event and he hoped the auction would start soon, because tonight was going to be extremely fun, exciting and with all the hot men here Scott really wanted to have some adult fun too.

***

8th November 2022

Classified Location, Southern France

Australian Secret Intelligence Service (ASIS) Officer Adamo Blackman had always found Europe a funny place filled with strange countries, strange people and extremely strange politics. And this entire castle with all the hot men and women walking around only seemed to prove his point even more.

Adamo had always grown up in Australia and that was the home he loved and treasured with all his heart, even if his slightly homophobic country didn't always care about him. But at the end of the day, he was always going to do whatever it took to protect Australia and its interests.

Adamo sat on a very old brown wooden chair

that was probably from the 1800s like the rest of the ancient tables and chairs and art on the bright white walls that surrounded him as Adamo focused on the dance floor a few metres from him.

He had to admit the chamber or dance floor or whatever the pompous French owners of this castle wanted to call it, was actually very nice. There were little stylish details on the walls, ceiling and everywhere that added such texture and depth to what would be a very dull chamber without it.

That was what Adamo really liked about Europe, they definitely knew how to make things interesting and now Adamo understood why all the top artists came from here.

And an added bonus was definitely all the hot French, Spanish and even Chilian men that were walking round in their expensive posh suits. Adamo had never given European men too many looks before, but given how many of them were young, hot as hell and very fit, Adamo was so going to change that opinion.

Adamo watched a youngish gay couple, clearly French, walk around pompously with their fingers wrapped round each other and no one seemed to care. Something else that Adamo had only ever encountered in Europe.

The breath-taking smells of sexy earthy aftershave hinted with cloves, forests and another refreshing scent that Adamo couldn't identify filled the air as the live band (which wasn't bad looking either) broke out into another song, and Adamo was so glad Australia wasn't as big on classical music as these Europeans.

Classical music was awful.

That was the reason why Adamo was rather simple and he really looking forward to the auction because his bosses as ASIS has given him 50 million euros to secure the information pertaining to Sarah Mckinnon.

Adamo seriously hated the damn woman especially after killing his best friend, almost killing him and just being a massive pain in the ass.

The English were such idiots for allowing her to live so long. Considering the British MI6 was meant to be the best in the world, unstoppable and extremely resourceful they were proving to be nothing short of pathetic.

Adamo had killed tons of rogue agents in his time whenever the ASIS required him to, and it was a really fun challenge but it wasn't impossible. Clearly the British couldn't have cared less about their rogue agent traveling the world, killing people and leaving nothing but wreckage in her wake.

Damn the British.

Adamo continued to scan the dance floor and he felt his stomach churn a little bit as he looked at all the hot men hugging, loving and dancing with their wives. It must have been nice for the hotties to do that so openly and in public without anyone caring.

Adamo had been gay or sometimes bisexual

depending on the woman and year for as long as he could remember, but even then growing up in rural Australia on his dad's farm wasn't exactly a paradise for a gay son, his dad's only son.

Adamo tried to force himself to smile at the memory of how disappointed, outraged and heartbroken his dad had been when Adamo had come out. His dad was so upset that he had lost his heir, he wasn't going to have any grandchildren and Adamo would be just as useless as his sister on the farm.

That was another thing that Adamo liked about Europe, it definitely had its problems but at least the sexism wasn't quite as blatant as it was in rural Australia, because Adamo's precious older sister was far from useless and Adamo still couldn't believe the entire family hadn't understood why she had fled to Italy when her boyfriend had given her the chance.

Adamo certainly understood now.

The live band turned slightly louder as they started playing some German rubbish and given how Adamo had been worried from the start about how intelligence agencies might come here to get the same information as him, Adamo looked up and started scanning the upper floor to see if anyone was doing the same as him.

Damn it.

Adamo's eyes immediately noticed an extremely cute boy the same age as him leaning on the dark brown wooden railing and staring down at the dance floor.

That might not have sounded like anything to worry about and that was exactly what Adamo would have told new recruits, but there was just something in those light brown eyes that Adamo recognised.

That cute boy was scanning the dance floor and trying to make it look like he was staring at the hot women (or hopefully men). Adamo had to admit the cute boy was good at pretending and Adamo had actually almost missed it.

Almost.

Adamo just kept staring at the cute boy and he really was cute. There was just something about how confidently the tall, fit, skinny boy stood that radiated happiness and authority and confidence from him that Adamo really respected.

The cute boy was wearing a very expensive and extremely flattering black suit, white crisp shirt and silky black trousers. The boy really did look so perfect and hot and his smooth handsome face was accented effortlessly by his brown hair in the faded style that Adamo had seen so men wear in Europe with the short hair expertly faded into longer hair on top.

He was beautiful.

But Adamo had to admit if this cute boy was a spy then he had to talk to the cutie, assess if he was a threat and then deal with him if he was.

Adamo really hoped that the cutie wasn't a threat because he was far too beautiful to be a danger.

Yet looks could be deceiving.

***

8th November 2022

Classified Location, Southern France

"Five minutes until the auction!" an elderly French man shouted in English.

Scott was so pleased to hear that the auction was finally going to happen as he leant against the warm dark brown wooden railing near a red-carpeted staircase that led down to the dance floor. Scott had spoken to a lot of French, Spanish and Chilian men and surprisingly enough he didn't even need to put on an accent, something he was extremely good at.

No one at all seemed to care that he was English and everyone had already guessed he was an intelligence officer after the information.

Scott wasn't exactly sure how comfortable he was with that fact because he was quickly learning that everyone here was current or former intelligence officers from their own countries.

Scott had fully believed this was a dodgy auction that was going to be filled with terrorists, criminals and more, but it turned out that the vast majority of people here were acting on behalf of their own governments. And Scott felt his stomach tense more and more at the idea of being trapped in a castle filled with so many professional killers, even his shoulders were tensing, something that never happened.

A whiff of strong sexy manly scent filled the air as someone leant against the railings next to Scott, and Scott could just tell that the man was pretending to focus on the dance floor below but he was really interested in him.

"You're too beautiful to be here by yourself," the man said.

Scott smiled and just looked at the man and... wow Scott couldn't believe how hot the man was.

Scott felt his stomach churn for a completely different reason now and all the tension in his shoulders, chest and body relaxed because all he could do was focus on the insanely gorgeous man standing less than a metre from him.

Scott seriously liked the cheap(ish) looking dark blue suit that told Scott instantly that the gorgeous man was an intelligence officer of some sort, but the beautiful suit really did highlight the gorgeous man's slight muscles, large arms and very fit body that Scott wouldn't have minded running his hands over to give the gorgeous man a quick pad down.

The gorgeous man's face was handsome, cute and it looked so caring in the light of the castle. He had a very slight golden blond beard that was accented by the man's blond crewcut, something that Scott hated on most men but this gorgeous man actually managed to make it work.

But what really did it for Scott was his gorgeous blue eyes that was like staring into the beautiful crystal blue ocean on the most perfect holiday imaginable.

"You really are too beautiful to be standing by yourself," the gorgeous man said. "You look cute, sweet and a little too innocent to be here too,"

Scott just smiled. This sexy man really was a

smooth talker.

"I'm Adamo," he said, and Scott just nodded as he realised that it was an Australian accent he was hearing.

And Scott had to almost catch himself before falling into the classic trap of why Adamo didn't talk like a typical Australian. It was simply because in Scott's experience it was always best to train out accents and dialects. It just made intelligence work a damn slight easier.

"So tell me," Scott said, "why is the…. Australian Secret Intelligence Service in France?"

Scott loved it how when Adamo smiled, his entire handsome face lit up.

"I was only being honest with you. I do think you're cute and beautiful and I can tell you're into me too,"

Damn it. Scott was normally a master of hiding whatever he was thinking whenever he was on a mission. He was known as being one of the calmest and coldest agents when he was on the job.

Scott had to focus and hide his thoughts better, he couldn't let this hottie read him.

Adamo moved closer and Scott hated it as his wayward parts sprung to life and Scott seriously had to fight the urge to move closer and kiss the sexy man only centimetres from him.

"My question," Scott said coldly.

Adamo shook his head. "I can tell you're into me and I know you aren't all work and no play. I can just tell that about you,"

Scott was impressed. This Officer was very good at changing the conversation, playing on Scott's feelings and making him focus on different things. That had to change.

"Did you realise that after Australia pulled out of that submarine deal in 2021 with France in exchange for AUKUS the French haven't been very tolerant of the ASIS?" Scott asked.

That made the hot smile on Adamo's face melt away slightly. "I am aware of that,"

"Then you are also aware that there are at least twenty DGSE agents here that I am sure would be all too happy to kick an ASIS agent out of their country," Scott said grinning.

Adamo rolled his eyes. "Fine, what do you want to know?"

Scott was so tempted to admit how badly he wanted this gorgeous man to take him to a nearby hotel and do him, and let them explore each other's bodies but Scott forced himself not to.

Damn it. Scott hated how he couldn't stop thinking about how beautiful and downright sexy Adamo was. He had to focus.

"Why is the ASIS here?"

"We're here to make sure the British don't fuck up another Sarah McKinnon mission," Adamo said. "Australia will get the information and then we will deal with Sarah personally,"

Scott almost laughed but he could hear the anger,

outrage and annoyance in Adamo's voice crystal clear, but then Adamo placed his perfectly warm and smooth hands on top of Scott's. Normally Scott would have recoiled instantly and hated the touch of someone else without him making the first move but surprisingly enough this actually felt… right, natural and really perfect.

"I'm sorry," Adamo said. "It's just that she killed my best friend, caused me a lot of problems and I just hate her,"

Scott nodded, he could understand that. He really could.

"Everyone," an elderly French man said. "The auction will now begin,"

As the man continued to explain the rules of the auction to everyone in the chamber and Adamo was focusing solely on the man. Scott just couldn't look down from Adamo.

He was so cute, gorgeous and Scott really, really wanted to get to know him better.

And he almost wished that he had met Adamo in another place in another city in another life because romances between intelligence officers never ended well.

And Scott really didn't want that to happen to him and Adamo but he wasn't sure it could be avoided.

***

8th November 2022

Classified Location, Southern France

Adamo was just flat out amazed at how weird the past two hours had been. When he had come to the auction and the castle he had of course known what was up for sale, how much people were willing to pay for these top-secret pieces of information and that some people might have even fight for it. But it had actually been rather calm.

Adamo stood right next to beautiful Scott at the very end of the lower level pressing his back against a wonderfully warm bright white wall, and right in front of him the red-carpeted dance floor had been transformed into a real auction with rows upon rows of dark brown wooden chairs with tons of posh and rich and snobby people sitting on them.

Adamo had been really impressed with Scott throughout all of it and he had actually learnt a lot about European relations and what each government was after and why it wasn't surprising who bided on what item. And Adamo had already spent 5 million of his euros on some classified Australian documents that detailed out where Australia's brand-new nuclear submarines were repaired, something that not even the British or Americans knew.

"And now the item we have all been waiting for," the elderly French man said who was standing at the front holding a thick folder.

Adamo leant forward slightly as everyone in the entire chamber fell silent as everyone just wanted confirmation that it contained the location of Sarah McKinnon, but the silence concerned Adamo a lot more than he ever wanted to admit.

He had no idea that there were so many people interested in the item and clearly this was going to get very expensive very quickly. And as beautiful, sexy and hot as Scott was he couldn't allow the British to get the information.

"I take it we're bidding against each other," Scott said with an evil grin.

But as Adamo looked into Scott's amazing light brown eyes with little flecks of whiskey thrown in to make them even more beautiful, Adamo could just tell there was sort of hurt in his voice.

And Adamo didn't want to bid against him either.

Adamo seriously liked Scott, and the past two hours had been wonderful as they had talked, laughed and made fun of each other's countries (respectfully of course) and it had even been magical. But a job was a job and sadly Adamo had to bid against Scott and stop the British from getting the information.

"You really are beautiful," Adamo said looking at the floor.

Scott hissed a little and clearly wasn't impressed, and a non-intelligence officer might have wondered why Scott didn't just avoid bidding altogether so Adamo could have it. But Adamo knew that MI6 never would have allowed that.

Both of their careers and governments had put them in an impossible position.

"Let's start the bidding at two million euros," the

auctioneer said.

"Ten million," a Spanish woman said.

"Twenty million," A Chilian man said.

Adamo really wasn't liking this at all. These prices were rising way too quickly for his liking.

"Thirty million," Scott said coldly.

The bid slammed into Adamo's ears like a hammer blow and Adamo was almost annoyed at himself for feeling like this in a way. He had been nothing but flirty, chatty and vulnerable all evening around Scott, something he never ever normally did.

"31 million," Adamo said.

Everyone laughed and Adamo instantly realised how poor he looked by only increasing it by 1 million.

"45 million," Adamo said.

Everyone went silent and Adamo looked at Scott and tried to smile. Scott weakly smiled back.

"51 million," a Russian woman said near the front.

"Damn it," Adamo said to Scott. "That's over my budget,"

Then Adamo realised if there was any way he was going to keep his job then he was going to have to use every trick in the book. He needed Scott and the British to give him some money.

"How much have you got?" Adamo asked.

Scott smiled. "I'm not telling you,"

"Please beautiful," Adamo said. "My job is at stake,

Scott shot Adamo a warning look. "Stop trying

to manipulate me. All you have done tonight is flirt with me, pull on my emotions and now you reveal your true intentions. You just want my money,"

Adamo covered his mouth with his hands. He had no idea that was how he was coming across. He hadn't meant it in the slightest.

"55 million," a Spanish man shouted.

Adamo really smiled at Scott. "Please Scott. I'm trying to not do anything to you and we need to put our governments aside or we will lose this auction,"

Adamo could see Scott was working through his options in his head. "Fine. But we don't open the folder until our bosses agree the takedown is a joint op,"

"Done," Adamo said.

"55 million," the auctioneer said. "Going once. Going Twice-"

"60 million euros!" Scott shouted.

Everyone gasped and everyone started shaking their heads.

"Sold to the British man at the back. Happy hunting and try not to fuck it up again," the auctioneer said as he handed the folder to a young woman in a black waitress' uniform.

Adamo hugged Scott and really loved how natural and right and wonderful the hug felt. Adamo seriously liked the feeling of Scott in his arms.

"Thank you," Adamo said. "How much did you have to play with?"

Scott grinned. "Fifty million euros and at least I

only spent 10,"

Adamo was about to start telling Scott how beautiful he looked again because he really did look it under the golden light of the chamber but he noticed that the young woman holding the folder was staring at them and she wasn't smiling.

"Tell me," Adamo said hugging Scott again and whispering into his ear, "does that young woman look like Sarah to you?"

Adamo gently turned Scott around so he could see the young woman and he felt Scott nod.

They both broke the hug and Adamo focused on the rather short young woman wearing the black waitress uniform. She was very small with her long glossy black hair that was almost certainly a wig but it was her strong jawline, thin waist and large arms that made her look like a former intelligence officer.

Adamo and Scott started to go over to her.

Adamo quickly realised they were completely unarmed without weapons, backup and Adamo seriously doubted any intelligence officer in the entire chamber would want to help them.

The young woman whipped out a pistol ran up to the elderly French man and put the gun to his head.

"Everyone leave!" Sarah shouted. "Except the brit and the Aussie,"

Everyone shrugged and Adamo just grabbed Scott's hand tight. Not as a sign of weakness or manipulation or anything besides from love pure and simple.

Because Adamo really didn't want anything to happen to Scott in the slightest. He was too precious for that.

***

8th November 2022

Classified Location, Southern France

When the entire red-carpeted chamber was empty except for Adamo and Scott and the hostage that Sarah was still aiming the gun at, Adamo realised that the entire item had been a mistake and the documents had probably been entered into the auction by Sarah herself so she could kill anyone hunting her.

"Why do you want us?" Adamo asked.

Scott shook off Adamo's hand and took a few steps forward.

"I wanted you both here because I wanted to send a message to the stupid Brits and Aussies," Sarah said. "Stop hunting me. I have my jobs to do and I have my people to kill,"

"What you are doing is wrong," Scott said.

Adamo really doubted a morality lesson was going to do much good here but he wanted Scott to buy him as much time as possible.

Adamo had to figure out a way to escape this mess.

"You see Aussie," Sarah said. "The Brits always say they're the good guys, defender of democracy and more but do you want to know how many elections I have rigged,"

Adamo shook his head. "We all do things for our countries we aren't proud of. It doesn't mean killing innocent people makes you any better,"

Sarah laughed and pressed the gun harder against her hostage's skull.

Adamo and Scott took a few steps closer until they were only ten metres away from her.

"Maybe you are right," Sarah said, "but if I leave here tonight killing the former head of the DGSE, a Brit and an Aussie then my world will be a lot safer,"

Adamo had wondered where he had recognised the auctioneer from.

Scott took a few more steps towards Sarah but she aimed the gun at Scott. Adamo's stomach tensed.

Sarah fired at Scott's feet.

"No!" Adamo shouted and rushed forward.

Sarah busted out laughing. "Seriously? An Aussie officer loving a brit. Wow,"

Adamo covered his mouth with his hands as he realised what he had done. He had given Sarah the perfect weapon to use against them both and when Scott looked at him it wasn't a hateful or regretful smile it was a look of concern for him too.

Because Scott would have done the exact same thing if Adamo had been in trouble.

Sarah fired. Shooting the auctioneer in the leg. She threw him to one side.

She aimed the gun at Scott. "Don't resist,"

Adamo nodded at Scott and he allowed Sarah to

put him in a headlock as he pressed the barrel of her gun against his head.

Adamo hated all of this he felt so useless, weak and unless he came up with something very quickly he was about to have the blood of an absolutely beautiful boy on his hands.

"Now this is going to be a bit more interesting," Sarah said. "I know you Scotty boy have another forty million euros. You're going to tell me the MI6 account number, password and you will authenticate my transaction when I drain the account,"

Scott laughed. "Never,"

Sarah hissed. She aimed the gun at Adamo.

"Fine then. Do it or he dies,"

"Let me die," Adamo said before he realised what he was saying. "Just let Scott live,"

Adamo was surprised at the anger in Scott's eyes like he was really pissed that Adamo was prepared to die for him.

"What's your answer?" Sarah asked Scott. "I will kill him,"

Adamo just looked at beautiful Scott just in case this was the last time he was going to see his handsome face.

"Never," Scott said with a hint of sadness and just winked at Adamo.

Adamo didn't know what Scott was planning but in all his years of experience he knew that time was an Officer's best friend.

"You know what bitch," Adamo shouted, "fuck

you and your fucking government. The British are just useless pricks that pretend to know what they're doing when they're just blind idiots,"

Adamo loved how Sarah's face twisted into confusion.

Scott stamped on her foot.

She screamed.

Adamo rushed forward.

Scott elbowed her in the ribs.

Sarah released him.

Adamo tackled her to the ground.

Slamming his fists into her head.

Police sirens came from outside.

"Internal Security," Scott said.

Adamo just looked at Sarah. He saw the gun a few metres away. It was their only option.

Scott picked up the gun. Aimed it at Sarah. Adamo nodded.

The bullet screamed through the air.

And Adamo instantly realised this was a hot handsome man he could always see himself working with because he really was beautiful and clever and perfect.

***

9th November 2022

Classified Location, Southern France

Scott was completely amazed at how wonderful the Directorate-General For Internal Security agents were when they had stormed into the chamber and because they had snapped up some of their own Most

Wanted because it seemed that the Chilian agents were not fans of the French whatsoever, the French really hadn't cared too much that MI6 and ASIS had killed someone in their country.

Scott was more than glad about that because the last thing he had wanted to do was had to fight the French and risk gorgeous Adamo getting hurt in the process, but Adamo really was an amazing man for what he had been willing to do to make sure he had lived.

Scott and Adamo stood in a very large field in the south of France with thick wonderful grass coming up to their ankles, a cool breeze blowing between them and messing up their hair and the pitch darkness of the field was illuminated slightly by the dazzling lights of a nearby French city.

France really was a beautiful country.

Even the air smelt perfectly refreshing with the tangy refreshing hints of autumn and Scott was slowly realising that he didn't actually want MI6 to come and pick him up from the extraction point, all Scott really wanted to do was spend just a little more time with the gorgeous boy he was starting to fall for.

The pitch darkness with the little illumination really didn't detract from Adamo's beauty. He was so fit, handsome and really had a beauty about him that Scott hadn't seen before, and it only took him a few more moments to realise that that beauty was that Adamo actually cared about him.

Something no one else had truly done before.

"Take this beautiful," Adamo said holding out a thick folder to Scott.

Scott knew exactly what it was, it was the Australian nuclear information that he had bought earlier, but he couldn't understand why Adamo wanted him to have it.

"No doubt it will come to light we fell for each other. Our governments won't like that and they'll get to kick you out," Adamo said, "because they'll be scared you're an Aussie turncoat or you're compromised,"

Scott nodded. It made sense and he could think of at least ten people back at MI6 that would try to kick him out because he was a lot better than them but he wasn't going to risk Australia's national security just to save his own skin. That wasn't right so that was exactly what he told Adamo.

"I don't want anything to happen to you because of what I did. If I wasn't so into you I wouldn't have revealed my feelings in front of a target. If it was better you could have arrested Sarah and got information from her. If I was better-"

Scott just kissed him.

Scott pressed his lips against Adamo's and was surprised how warm, smooth and lustrous they were. He had been wanting to kiss this gorgeous man for so long and now he was finally doing it, it felt so right.

"You're perfect the way you are," Scott said breaking the kiss and gently running his hands up and down Adamo's body.

Adamo's body really did feel as amazing as Scott had dreamed.

"What will you do now?" Scott asked.

Adamo smiled. "The ASIS has interests all over the globe. Europe, the Americas and Asia all have threats against Australia. Maybe we'll even meet each other again officially or not,"

As the distant sound of a helicopter got closer and closer Scott knew that his time was running out but surprisingly enough didn't feel as sad as he had earlier. Because he knew he would see gorgeous Adamo again on another mission in another country away from the eyes of their governments.

And at the end of the day, the UK and Australia were close allies and allies really did need to work *closely* together in these dark times and sometimes so close that skin and wayward parts would touch.

Scott knew it wouldn't be a hard sell to his or Adamo's bosses and Scott was seriously looking forward to a wonderful future of working with this gorgeous man who he had really fallen for in the past few hours.

The future was going to be amazing and bright and wonderful so Scott gave Adamo a final deep passionate kiss as the MI6 helicopter landed.

And Scott left Adamo. Definitely not for the last time because they would soon see each other again and Scott fully intended to pick up exactly where they left off.

DEMOCRACY WORKS

MI5 Officer Finley Boddy had always loved how amazing democracy was. It gave the amazing, wonderful people of a country the chance to have their say, choose their leaders and actually have an input into how they wanted their rulers to impact their lives. It was just such an amazing way to run a country and Finley seriously felt sorry for any country unfortunate enough not to have their absolutely brilliant governance system.

And Finley was going to do anything in his power to keep UK democracy working.

Finley sat in his little black car with the heating on full blast to keep himself warm and toasty and ready for action. He had parked his little car on a long wide road filled with potholes, broken street lamps and overflowing rubbish bins, but Finley wouldn't have it any other way.

As he looked at all the abandoned warehouses that lined the road with their wire fences rusting away and getting broken into more times than not, Finley was so excited to be here.

The road thankfully wasn't completely empty as there were about ten other cars parked on the road but all of those had smashed windscreens, stolen hubcaps and some even had their cars stolen. Yet that was all good because at least it sort of gave Finley a little bit more camouflage in case anyone in those warehouses and so-called abandoned factories saw him.

Tonight was a perfect night for intelligence work with it being pitch black, icy cold and there was no one about. Finley could probably run, dance and scream down the road without anyone paying attention to him or even noticing he was here.

But that was too much of a risk.

Finley might have preferred to be at the gym tonight working on his body (to make sure he had the strength required for his job, not for vanity reasons) but he had had a leg day yesterday, or maybe he could have been working on his amateur gymnastic routines which he was amazingly good at, or maybe he could have gone to some gay clubs in London or Kent to meet a cute boy.

But he loved intelligence work and democracy far too much for any of that to stop him coming out tonight.

And Finley was really glad that his vegan chia latte was sending beautiful hints of cinnamon, bitter coffee and sweet sugary scents into the air and it made the delightful taste of cookie form on his tongue. It was so nice to smell something good for a change considering how bad the car stunk when MI5 had first given it to him.

It was so cold outside that Finley was surprised that the little black car that MI5 had given him for this mission hadn't frozen or failed to start because it was so icy. Finley had been concerned about the engine coolant getting frozen but he had to admit that MI5 was better than that.

Even the icy cold silence of the road Finley was watching was a great change from all the constant noise, chaos and business of London and the other cities that Finley normally worked in.

But Finley just couldn't help but feel this was nothing more than the calming silence before the storm.

And Finley was so excited about this mission because it combined everything he loved about the UK.

Because with there being a general election tomorrow to decide who would be the next Prime Minister for the next four years (or matter of weeks as that was the trend these days) MI5, 6 and all the other UK intelligence agencies weren't officially allowed to get involved in politics, but for the sake of democracy they were running a very covert op.

Finley had jumped at the chance to be here tonight because one of these warehouses was meant to be a Russian computer centre where they created fake news, uploaded it straight into the UK critical infrastructure and fed all their hate, despise and propaganda into the UK media for the people to consume.

Finley seriously hated the Russians with all of his heart because they were the massive threat to his beloved democracy and they were a threat to everything he had fought so hard to protect over the years. The Russians were just foul, disgusting and outrageous people that needed to suffer for their crimes against democracy.

Finley had been sitting in the car for about two hours now and he just couldn't get the horrible crimes out of his mind. It was too disgusting to imagine that inside one of these warehouses, the Russians were doing such awful things to his democracy and chances are the current government would stay in power.

And Finley fully respected that some in MI5 thought that was a good thing, but everyone in the intelligence community had seen the leaked documents about how much further right the government was going to move, and their new election campaign promised three simple things.

The repealing of gay rights, repealing benefits and giving all illegal immigrants a life sentence of hard labour.

Of course under international law a number of these three things were illegal and Finley was just concerned about himself more than anything else. He had read plenty of stories from his fellow gay friends in other countries, he didn't want to be illegal just because he loved another man and Finley seriously hated the whole anti-immigrant stance of the UK.

Finley had checked the data recently at MI5 and it was just amazing how 84% of whoever came to the UK was legally allowed to set here because they were real immigrants and they wanted to work and pay tax. But clearly politicians didn't like data and real numbers but that was why this mission was so important.

Because so many lives, lifestyles and democracy itself rested on Finley helping to make sure the current government failed.

And Finley seriously didn't want to be illegal like all those that came before him had to suffer through.

***

Private Security Contractor and Former GCHQ Officer Hunter Muffin was so glad to finally be rid of bloody GCHQ, the UK's version of the US's NSA, because during the five years he had loyally worked for them, he had seen so many attacks, cyberattacks and disinformation campaigns than he ever cared to think about, and all GCHQ could do was sit on their backsides and protect the UK through computer work. Which was extremely useful and Hunter loved his fellow geeks for that but sometimes action and gunfights needed to happen to really protect the UK.

And Hunter was just glad he could do it.

Hunter stood on the edge of an icy cold alley

with dirty brick walls either side of him with ripped down posters of something or another and bins were overflowing but he was more than glad the alley didn't smell at all.

In fact Hunter had made sure he had picked a hiding spot that didn't smell awful, and at least the air was damp, crisp and almost refreshing instead of smelly. That was something Hunter really didn't want to have to deal with.

Out ahead of Hunter was a long dark road that was mostly illuminated only by the moonlight as all the streetlamps, that were an even ten metres apart, on road were broken and he wouldn't have been surprised in the local council had cut the power to this area years ago, maybe even a decade. That was how unloved the area looked.

Thankfully with the rather wonderful moon being full tonight, it gave Hunter plenty of light to study his surroundings and formulate a plan. All Hunter could focus on was the massive rusting warehouse in front of him because that was his target.

The warehouse from the outside looked to be completely rusted and wrecked with massive chunks of the metal cladding on the outside being torn away in the wind, rain and the roof hardly looked any better.

But Hunter had seen people coming and going for days and nights and even takeaway deliverers (which Hunter had posed as) were receiving plenty of orders. When Hunter had been inside, he was surprised to see that everyone was English in the warehouse and it hardly seemed like any foreign powers were involved, that was surprising considering it was almost always Russia who was behind these sort of misinformation campaigns.

Hunter hated the silence of the road. It wasn't natural and Hunter seriously preferred the nosiness of London and the other cities that his private contractor firm had sent him to, Canterbury in the south of England was probably his favourite but the silence here was just annoying.

The only good thing about the silence was that at least he could be able to hear if anyone was sneaking up on him.

Hunter edged forward slightly and focused for a moment on the eleven cars that were parked on the road. Normally he would have been glad to see so many parked cars with broken windscreens, stolen hubcaps and some had stolen wheels but Hunter knew that a car had joined this lot since yesterday.

And that was so annoying and very dangerous.

Hunter already hated the people inside this warehouse enough because they were trying to divide democracy, people and keep the ever-moving-further-right government in power. Something he seriously didn't want as the government was coming after gay rights next then ethnic minorities and then women.

It was just utterly pathetic that even in the 21st century people still believed that the morals and laws of the 19th century were still perfectly okay and we had to return to them to protect the "fabric" of society, whatever the fuck that meant.

But Hunter didn't entirely blame the politicians for this mess.

Hunter really blamed democracy for it all because whilst it was always far, far better than the alternative of a dictatorship. Democracy was far from perfect because to Hunter it just seemed like people were choosing politicians over their personality and how outrageous they were. Instead of what was right for themselves, their families and the country.

Maybe it had always been like that but Hunter just hated how people were voting for politicians who wanted to destroy groups just because they were white, straight, rich and powerful.

Hunter shook his head because he couldn't focus on his mild distaste for democracy because there was a mission to do, a country to save and a disinformation campaign to stop.

A car door slammed shut.

Hunter crouched down and focused on the long line of cars that were parked on the road. He saw a man start to walk towards him but the moonlight was far too poor to let Hunter see his face.

Hunter was going to have to grab him. If it was an innocent person then Hunter would just let them go, if it was an enemy Hunter would knock him out and arrest him later and if it was another UK intelligence agency, then Hunter really didn't know what he would do.

As far as Hunter was concerned all the UK intelligence agencies were as weak as each other when it came to protecting the UK's integrity. All the agencies knew the challenges and risks and dangers the government posed to the UK but because they were "elected" no one wanted to do anything about it.

Yet another drawback of democracy.

Hunter stood up and pressed his back against the icy cold brick wall of the alley and waited for the person to walk past.

Hunter heard the man's footsteps get closer.

The man walked past.

Hunter grabbed him. Slamming the man against the wall. Covering his mouth with his hands.

Hunter slammed his arm against the man's throat and looked at the… wow.

The man Hunter was currently pinning against the wall was actually really beautiful, gorgeous and damn well attractive. The man was wearing a very well-fitting black overcoat that highlighted how fit, sexy and toned he was and Hunter was so tempted to give him a little pad down to cop a feel, but he forced himself not to.

The gorgeous man also looked so cute with his smooth white face, pointy chin that only seemed to make him seem even cuter and it was actually like the gorgeous man's face was a perfect seductive blend of masculinity and femininity.

That perfectly seductive blend was only accented wonderfully by the man's longish black hair that was going curly and cute and really made the man seem so innocent.

Hunter accidentally kneed the gorgeous man and he instantly felt the cold hard impression of a gun at the man's waist.

Now Hunter was just wondering why the hell was such a cute man creeping about abandoned warehouses with a gun late at night?

And whatever the answer was it just concerned Hunter a lot more than he ever wanted to admit.

***

Finley actually had no problem whatsoever with being thrown about by cute sexy men, it was something that his ex-boyfriends had done plenty of times before but there was just something about this man that seriously captured Finley's imagination.

Finley was even a little turned-on by the fact the hot man had his arm across Finley's throat but he was pushing against it and with each passing second the pressure seemed to be getting less and less.

Even the icy coldness of the brick wall behind him and the entire dirty alley wasn't too bad and now there was a hot man involved this was nowhere as bad as it could have been.

As the hot man took his rough hand off Finley's mouth, he just smiled at the hot man because he really was hot. The man didn't look like a Russian or anyone who would want to harm wonderful democracy and he clearly wasn't the fighting type.

Finley seriously doubted he was even a real

intelligence officer because Finley didn't see any indication of toned muscle judging by the outline of his skin-tight hoody, black jeans and hiking boots. There clearly wasn't any fat on the hot man's body but he wasn't muscular either, something he had learnt to expect from intelligence officers.

But Finley was a lot more interested in the hot man's handsome face with his short brown hair cut in a crewcut style that really worked on this hottie, and Finley couldn't look away from the hottie's strong jawline, round chin and very beautiful emerald eyes with little flecks of sapphire mixed in.

"Who are you?" the hottie asked like the very act of speaking was painful for him.

Finley was more than grateful his throat had dried up but he was a little annoyed that sweat was dripping off his back. He just hoped this hottie wouldn't notice.

"MI5 Finley Boddy," he said.

Damn it that was such a stupid thing to do Finley realised, he never should have identified himself and normally he never did. He especially shouldn't have said that when the hottie was still pinning him against the wall.

What the hell was this hottie doing to him?"

Thankfully the hottie released him and Finley vowed not to keep doing stupid things in front of the insanely hot man.

"I didn't think MI5 and the other agencies were bothering with this threat," the hottie said.

Finley smiled. "Some of us are even if it is illegal and outside of our remit,"

The hottie slowly nodded and Finley could tell he was a little confused but glad about him being here at the same time.

"Who are you?" Finley asked, really hoping this hottie wasn't a foreign agent or something else that would only complicate matters.

"Hunter Muffin, former GCHQ and now a private contractor," the hottie said.

Finley smiled because he had been sure this guy definitely wasn't a real intelligence officer and that really made him feel good if this man was a danger to his precious democracy then there was a good chance Finley could take him.

Finley looked over to the warehouse that he had been walking to when beautiful Hunter had grabbed him.

"There's no security on the outside," Hunter said. "I don't see any cameras and there was more than enough holes in the wire fences for us to go through,"

Finley nodded and it was clear that Hunter had been here for a while if he was able to get this much information. "How long?"

"Two days really maybe three," Hunter said. "The company I work for learnt about the threat and I was assigned to stop it before the *election*,"

Finley looked at Hunter a little more as he said *election* with such disdain.

"You don't like elections?" Finley asked knowing it was impossible for people not to like them.

Hunter laughed and Finley's heart skipped a few beats, Hunter's laughter was so sweet, beautiful and lyrical. Finley really wanted to hear it again.

"I suggest we work together on this," Hunter said. "What backup do you have or equipment?"

Finley's mouth dropped a little at how bad he felt whenever he spoke to private contractors because they always had the private money, investment and research and development departments to get all the cool gadgets.

Finley just got out his gun. "That's my backup and that's my only equipment,"

Hunter looked like he was about to laugh, which Finley wanted so badly, but Hunter only nodded his head slowly.

Now Finley felt like such an idiot again because this damn beautiful man was bringing out all of his insecurities about his work.

Smoke bombs rained down on them.

Finley heard heavy footsteps come at him.

Someone grabbed him.

Finley punched them.

He hit body armour.

Finley jumped into the air.

Kicking out his legs.

He cracked a helmet.

More people charged at him.

Finley hated the smoke.

His eyes watered.

Smoke was clawing at his throat.

Someone grabbed Finley.

Throwing him against the wall.

Finley's head slammed into it.

Finley's world went black.

***

Of all the ways how Hunter wanted to spend his night, it certainly hadn't been stripped naked and tied to a stunningly beautiful man he had only just met. Now this wouldn't have been all bad but Hunter had been tied to sexy Finley with their fronts and wayward parts touching.

Hunter had only just woken up but it was very annoying because he was seriously enjoying the breath-taking view of Finley's very toned and hot and insanely beautiful body but Hunter's wayward part was trapped against something and he was in a little bit of pain down there.

Hunter managed to look around to see there were in the middle of a massive warehouse that was easily a hundred metres long and wide and there were a group of people typing, swirling and shouting at computers around them.

"Complete the data transfer," a man with a deep voice said.

But what really concerned Hunter was that the computers the people were sitting at were all leading to hundreds if not thousands of servers and that reminded Hunter of why he had really wanted to come on the mission.

Part of GCHQ's mandate was to protect the UK's critical infrastructure and right under this warehouse was a massive superfast internet cable transferring insane amounts of data from mainland Europe to the UK and right into the heart of London.

It was clear as day as the groups of people were using these computers to pour information right into cables and feed it into the UK internet framework. And Hunter just knew if the criminals really wanted to then it wouldn't be difficult for them to feed so much data through the cables to cause an overload and cause all of the UK's internet framework and infrastructure to shut down.

As beautiful Finley started to stir, Hunter just hated these bastards for attacking them like that and risking sexy Finley's life. And why the hell these criminals had stripped them both naked was beyond him but out of the corner of his eye Hunter did manage to see their clothes in two neat piles.

"Good to see you both awake," the man with the horrible deep voice said.

Hunter smiled weakly at Finley as he woke up and Hunter laughed a little as he felt Finley's wayward parts spring to life too.

They were clearly both into each other and Hunter really wanted to ask this cutie out on a real date.

"Why strip us?" Finley asked.

"Because I like hot men," the man said, "and my

workers deserve a little show after all of their hard work, and thank you for tipping me off Officer Boddy with your door slamming,"

Hunter just looked at Finley and he could tell how guilty he felt.

"What work are you doing here?" Hunter asked looking around to see if there was a way out.

"I thought you would appreciate what I'm doing Former Officer Muffin, you do hate elections, democracy and politicians after all,"

Hunter looked at Finley and he was amazed as Finley looked horrified at him and like he was the worst person in the entire world. And even though Hunter had never ever felt guilty for his views before, he felt like utter shit because the last thing he ever wanted to be was a monster in Finley's eyes.

"I don't hate democracy," Hunter said. "I just hate how people keep voting us towards damnation,"

Hunter was so glad that Finley sort of nodded.

A loud humming sound echoed around the warehouse and Hunter found him and Finley were being lifted up and turned to face the man with the deep voice.

Hunter instantly spat at the man's feet and he hated the middle-aged man with his baggy jeans, white crisp shirt and black Chelsea boots.

"I don't care why you do or don't," the man said. "I hate the UK too and that's why I keep steering it towards damnation and the best thing about it all is that you're right. The people do just keep voting for what I want them to do,"

Hunter felt Finley's sexy body shiver with fear.

"The people don't question the information they see. They don't care if politicians are honest or not. You were right the entire time Hunter. As long as people see a big personality that shouts and screams at so-called weaker people then they get their vote," the man said.

Hunter hated how this man knew exactly the point he had raised in the past to his friends and family about the failures of democracy but also the immense benefits.

"How long have you been watching me?" Hunter asked.

The man shrugged. "Maybe four years. You have given me a lot of good content to frame you with,"

Hunter and Finley's eyes just widened and they both instantly understood what this idiot was planning. Hunter couldn't believe the man was going to frame him for all of it.

Then Hunter focused on all the massive computers, small groups of people and all the electronics that could possibly burst into flames and cook them both alive.

If these people were smart enough to pour fake news and information into internet cables then it wouldn't have been hard for them to tell the computer's cooling fans to turn off. Then it could only be a matter of time before the computers caught alight and killed him and beautiful Finley in the process.

"How much longer until the data transfer is done?" the man asked.

"Done in two minutes boss. The transfer is fully automated. Can we go now?" a young woman asked.

"Of course," the man said.

He whipped out Finley's gun. Shooting all the other people in the head.

Hunter hissed. He hated he was chained up and locked in a warehouse with a madman with a gun.

"You see cuties," the man said. "I have laid out all the evidence to show that you Mr Muffin were behind the attack itself and the cyberattack that is going to cripple the opposition's computer systems and pump out so much hatred that all the stupid left-wingers and centralists will have to vote far-right because it will look like the only sane option,"

Hunter spat at this idiot again.

"And it will look like you Mr Boddy have killed all your workers to hide your tracks and all this evidence of mine will be released at the same time as the cyberattack,"

Hunter just looked at beautiful Finley. They didn't have a lot of time to escape, kill this madman and stop the cyberattack.

And that was all against the ticking clock of the computer fans being turned off and catching light.

"Before I go," the man said going over to one of the computers.

The computer exploded.

The man screamed. His face was engulfed in flames.

Seconds later his corpse slammed onto the ground.

More computers exploded. Flames roared in the distance.

Hunter and Finley had to escape now. There was no more time to mess around.

***

Hunter absolutely hated that stupid pathetic man who was so stupid that he was now nothing more than a smouldering corpse behind them.

Hunter had to escape before the burning computers cooked him and beautiful Finley alive. Or choked them to death on the toxic fumes now filling the air.

He really focused on what was tying him and Finley together. Hunter had been caught on being tied to such a beautiful guy before and that disgusting middle-aged man but now Hunter had to focus.

Their legs were tied together with rope that wasn't too thick or thin. Ideally they could snap the rope with their leg muscles but Hunter wasn't strong enough for that.

Their chests and stomachs were tied together with the same sort of rope but it was a lot thinner.

The real problem was Hunter and Finley's arms were pulled up over their heads and tied to some kind of pulley above them using very thick rope. Hunter was certain they could break that.

Another computer exploded.

The rope around their legs snapped.

"Thank God yesterday was leg day," Finley said.

Hunter wanted to kiss this hot sexy man more than anything.

"How are we gonna get rid of the stomach and chest ropes?" Hunter asked.

"You need to stay perfectly still for me," Finley said.

Hunter had no clue what Finley was talking about. More computers bursted into flames. Choking black smoke filled the warehouse.

Finley jumped up and jammed his knees against Hunter's knees and he started to move up and down.

Hunter quickly realised Finley was using his core strength to push his legs against Hunter making the rope stretch and hopefully snap.

The chest and stomach rope snapped.

"Excellent body by the way," Hunter said.

Finley grinned. "Not so bad yourself,"

Now they were free Hunter pulled his biceps to pull himself upwards so he could look at the pulley they were tied to.

The smoke was getting thicker and thicker. Hunter could barely see it.

Hunter's biceps hurt. They felt like he was being stabbed.

Hunter just didn't want to even imagine how close the cyberattack was close to launching.

"Let me," Finley said.

Hunter just watched as the beautiful man pulled himself upwards like a gymnast and wrapped his feet around the metal cable the pulley was hanging from.

Finley pulled himself up so he was artfully hanging from the metal cable and he smashed his fists into it.

Hunter dropped to the floor with a thud.

Finley screamed.

He fell to the ground.

He didn't move.

Hunter rushed over.

More computers exploded. Popped. Banged. Hunter checked Finley was breathing. He was.

Only just.

Hunter wanted to just run out of the warehouse with him.

He had to stop the cyberattack first.

The black smoke was so thick now. The roar of flames was deafening.

Hunter felt the flames lick his flesh.

Hunter went forward. He found a massive computer still working. It was showing 98% on the screen.

He rushed over to it. Hunter looked for an abort function.

There wasn't one.

The computer burst into flames. The glass screen exploded.

Shards sliced into Hunter's stomach.

He just knew that wouldn't stop the attack and

get him arrested.

Hunter quickly rushed round the back of the computer. It was connected to a strange black box device with massive cables pouring out of it.

It looked like something someone would use to attach the computer to servers.

Hunter realised the servers weren't connected to the massive cable connecting Europe to London. It was the computer and the servers were feeding the information to the computer through the black box device.

Hunter went over to it. He grabbed it. It was burning hot.

He screamed in agony.

Hunter threw it to the ground.

He smashed down on it.

Shattering it.

The burning hot material melted onto his foot. He screamed.

Hunter wiped as much as he could away.

Hunter had to get out.

He charged over to Finley. Scooping him up in his arms.

Hunter rushed towards the exit.

There was no chance to find their clothes. It was too late.

As Hunter just charged as fast as he could out of the burning warehouse Hunter really hoped the cyberattack was over and most importantly the beautiful man in his arms was alive.

***

It was four hours after the polls had closed the next day so it was two o'clock in the morning as Finley sat with the most beautiful guy he had ever met before. He was so glad that he hadn't inhaled too much smoke and besides the minor burns to his body and the cuts from the fall this little incident shouldn't have any lasting impacts.

But as Finley wrapped his arms around beautiful, hot, sexy Hunter, he really hoped this little incident would have a lasting impact on both of them, as they both sat on the icy cold edge of a glass balcony in one of London's tallest buildings.

From Hunter's wonderful apartment that the balcony belonged to, Finley could see the breathtaking skyline of London with all of its skyscrapers, weird buildings and bright stunning lights that really made London so beautiful, perfect and very, very precious.

Finley could even see the River Thames coursing through the darkness below them, and it really had been a wonderful night between them both. As soon as Finley had got out of hospital, he had phoned Hunter and wanted to meet, Hunter had cooked them both the most amazing mouth-watering meal of juicy crispy vegan chicken burgers, golden chips and creamy vegan vanilla ice cream Finley had ever had. Then they had spent the entire night talking, hugging and really getting to know each other.

But they hadn't kissed, spoken about the future

or even the election that was currently being counted. Because if what the madman in the warehouse had said was true about Hunter then Finley really didn't want to spoil tonight by talking about it.

Finley hugged Hunter even more and Finley loved the feeling of Hunter's thin body under his black hoodie and Finley really felt like a teenager again, that was something he hadn't felt for a long time.

And it felt utterly wonderful to have that feeling back.

"Who was that guy in the end?" Hunter asked quietly as he turned to look at Finley, and Finley really loved staring into Hunter's large adorable eyes.

"You knew I would have MI5 look him up," Finley said. "His name was Jude Griffins a former MI6 operative from the 80s and someone who learnt very quickly that the intelligence agencies of the UK were a little thick and the UK had betrayed him a total of five times and Jude had finally had enough,"

Finley really didn't want to get into the horrific details about how the UK had allowed the Iranians, North Koreans and Russians to capture Jude and torture him before they released him. but judging by Hunter's frown he ready knew or could guess what had happened.

"And then he wanted to destroy the UK and torture it like the enemy tortured him," Hunter said.

Finley just nodded because he sort of felt like Hunter wanted to make a point. "You can say it,"

Hunter smiled at him and Finley seriously couldn't get enough of his perfect smile. "I won't make me point, but why, why do you love democracy so much to the point of obsession? I like it, I do, but I accept it has massive weaknesses,"

Finley pulled Hunter closer to him. "So do I but without democracy what the hell are we? We're no better than China, Russia or the people we fight every single day to stop,"

Hunter slowly nodded.

"And I choose to believe no matter how stupid some of these governments are that get into power. Reason, rationality and hope will prevail. Like the current government, sure they will get in again but not with as much power as they did before. And that is only possible because…"

Hunter laughed his beautiful laugh again.

"Because of democracy. Some people realised this government is stupid and not serving them so they will vote for someone else,"

Hunter slowly nodded. "But how much damage will this government do before they're voted out for good? That is what I despair about,"

Finley ran his fingers through Hunter's wonderful hair and wanted so badly to kiss him. "I don't know but democracy will prevail and sooner or later they will be gone for good. Just you wait,"

Finley laughed his beautiful, sexy, lyrical laugh again and Finley's wayward parts sprung to life.

Hunter bit his lip. "I love your optimism. I like

you a lot. And I seriously like your body,"

Finley shivered in delight as Hunter carefully ran his fingers down Finley's clothes and stop just short of his belly button.

"You're such a tease," Finley said getting so close to Finley that their noses touched.

"Why don't you show me some of your gymnastic skills in my bedroom and we'll see what happens from there?" Hunter asked.

Finley just kissed him.

And moaned in sheer delight and pleasure and attraction as he felt the strength and wonderful passion behind the kiss. Hunter was really into him, and Finley was seriously into Hunter.

As Finley jumped into the air, wrapped his legs round Hunter's waist and Hunter carried him off to the bedroom, Finley just knew tonight and tomorrow were going to be utterly amazing.

And he really knew that they were going to be seeing each other for a long time after tomorrow. He just had an amazing feeling.

And as much as Finley knew Hunter would hate to admit it, they only met, fell in love and were together because democracy worked and that was far from a lie.

ROMANCE SPIES COLLECTION VOLUME 2

SPYING FOR INDEPENDENCE

MI5 Intelligence Officer Nick Blackford stood in one of London's massive ancient libraries with immensely beautiful floor-to-ceiling bookshelves, a dark and rather stunning hardwood floor and Nick really enjoyed the small crystal chandeliers that looked like they were floating down from the ceiling every ten metres. The entire library was a stunning array of engineering and as much as the English hated to admit that a Scottish person designed it, one did.

Nick loved looking through the great books on the shelves because this place wasn't exactly a public library because it was mainly reserved for lawyers, governmental people and other civil servants. Yet it was interesting to say the least how many erotica titles were on the shelves in amongst hardcore romance, spy novels and political thrillers.

Of course there were other so-called more important books in the library but Nick was only interested in the fiction part. That was thankfully where there were so few people walking about, there were only three people in the section that seemed to stretch on for a good twenty metres. Nick would have loved to count how many erotica titles there were in this aisle alone.

But he didn't have the time, or the inclination.

The other three people in the isle were only civil servants, wearing black suits, trousers and all of them had their white ID cards hanging around their neck, working for the UK government so they were hardly a threat, and Nick just needed somewhere local to meet a target and hopefully hack their phone to hopefully stop an awful terrorist attack against the nation of Scotland.

Just like all the other Scottish people, Nick had no problem with the English. The English were kind, helpful and even their weird tea obsessions didn't bother Nick and his fellow Scots, but he just didn't want to be ruled by them.

Nick had wanted Scotland to have its own government that could actually do whatever it wanted in the interest of its people instead of being told by the UK Government what it is was and wasn't allowed to do.

Nick really loved the smell of old libraries because they always had that sensational musty book smell about them, but this also had amazing scents of flowers, lavender and more fruity scents that were presumably coming from the civil servants' aftershaves and perfumes, leaving the wonderful taste of pizza like he had on hot summer evenings with his family a few years ago on his tongue.

When Nick had been working for MI5 yesterday looking through all the buried intelligence reports, the sort of reports that were deemed serious enough to keep a tab on but not serious enough to actually act on, Nick was rather surprised to see three analysts had picked up chatter about a probable terrorist attack against the Scottish people.

But it had been buried.

Now Nick had worked for MI5 for twenty years, he had stopped assassination attempts, he had protected the Welsh, English and Scots from various threats. Nick had never really done much for the Northern Irish but that was just because he had never got those cases. And never in those twenty years and hundreds of cases had Nick ever seen a terrorist attack getting buried.

And it was even worse that the disappeared file had implicated a Supreme Court Justice as one of the people supporting the terror attack.

Nick mentioned it to his supervisor of course, but she dismissed it as him making things up and when Nick went back to his computer the file and report and all remaining evidence of the plot had disappeared.

Nick was just grateful to have a photographic memory so he knew that the source of the chatter was a Supreme Court Justice and that's where things got very complicated apparently according to his Scottish-hating, English Patriotic work "friend" George Ashley.

Apparently MI5 was never going to contact or interview a Supreme Court Justice no matter if terrorist chatter mentioned them as a source, the donator to the terrorists or even helping the terrorists in any material way. All of that was of course illegal but apparently no one at MI5 actually cared about that.

Nick wasn't going to say to anyone outright that his boss and work "friends" at MI5 were trying to cover up something or play down the threat because they would rather deal with a more "important" threat, but he was certainly wanting to.

And at the end of the day, what were a few Scottish lives compared to English ones?

Nothing.

Nick really wanted the Supreme Court Justice to turn up to the library soon because Nick just wanted to get to the truth.

Whatever it was.

***

Michael had no idea his life would be changed for the better today.

MI5 Intelligence Officer Michael Ratlings went into the library that was reserved for only the finest civil servants, other governmental workers and lawyers in all of London. It was just amazing to Michael how massive this place was, of course it was a complete waste of space, money and manpower because Michael had no idea why these people couldn't use public libraries, instead of sapping public money away from more important things. Like hospitals.

But that was life.

Michael had to admit that the library did have beautifully long bookshelves that stretched right up to the ceiling and seemed to go back tens of metres. When he had been in law school he would have loved to have a library like this one, especially as this particular library had a copy of every single government Act that the UK Parliament had ever passed.

That was a lot of legal knowledge, power and resources in one place. And Michael really would have loved this when he was younger.

There was a small group of very young men and women standing over a massive ancient book, dressed in black trousers, shoes and very flattening dresses, and they were gasping about the content and everything. That was a great thing to see and Michael actually smiled at it.

After working as an intelligence officer for over twenty years, it was amazing to see that the youth of today were still interested in learning, growing and reading as much as he had been when Michael was that young.

Even the smell of the library was sensational with the musty smell of real books but he definitely didn't like the scents of cloves, coffee and other spices from people's aftershaves and perfumes. That was just wrong and it felt like they were invading the precious library space.

As much as Michael wanted to stay and look and read at all the books in the library, Michael had a job to do because he had to stop a rogue MI5 agent from doing something stupid.

Nick Blackford had gone rogue today after deleting important terrorist files that would help protect the UK Government and UK Prime Minister. Michael's bosses had already told him that Nick was an extremist that had already infiltrated the very top levels of UK government security.

And that was just typical of Scots.

Michael didn't have anything against Scottish people but most of them were bat crap crazy. Because Michael just couldn't understand why the nutters wanted independence from the UK, the UK might not have been a powerful country anymore, had massive political problems and was entering a massive recession, but to breakaway was stupid.

The Scots had joined the United Kingdom 400 years ago and there was no reason to change that.

But clearly this particular nutter didn't agree, so if what his bosses said was true then this Nick Blackford was going to assassinate a Supreme Court Justice, which made sense because the UK Supreme Court Justice was set to make a legal ruling tomorrow saying if the nutters could have yet another referendum on Independence.

Michael slowly started to make his way through the library, passing aisle of bookshelves after bookshelves. There were so many people inside the library with their different business clothes that it was impossible to see who was who.

But Nick Blackford was hunting down a Supreme Court Justice so that was who Michael had to find. He couldn't let the terrorist kill an innocent person and it was a terribly kept secret that all Justices loved erotica.

So Michael went over to the Erotica section and... oh, Michael realised he was in a lot of trouble.

Michael's heart pounded faster. Michael tripped over a little. Michael's throat was as dry as a desert.

All of this morning Michael had studied every single little piece of information about Nick Blackford, and Michael had looked at his picture plenty of times, but to actually see Nick Blackford in the flesh that was unreal.

Nick Blackford was just standing there reading a book in a long sexy black overcoat that made him look so stunningly beautiful. He was wearing a very well-fitting black suit underneath it that made Michael know that he was extremely fit and not packing a gun.

But he was certainly packing a lot of other goodness.

Michael bit his lip because it was just a shame that the terrorists were always the hot ones.

And this terrorist needed to be dealt with just like all the others.

Michael carefully took out his pistol, went over to Nick and forced the pistol into his side.

And this just felt so so wrong.

***

"Don't move," a man said.

Now Nick had been tortured by Russians in London, the Chinese in Wales and even some extreme versions of the Irish Republic Army in Birmingham, but never ever had been he been held at gunpoint in the middle of a semi-private library in the heart of London with three civil servants just next to him.

It was clear as day that this man was MI5 so Nick was a lot more interested in what lies this man had been told about him and what he was up to. Nick knew he shouldn't have taken a day off work to go hunting on this project but he was never going to let hurt innocent people, regardless of their nationality, to be hurt.

Even if the English wanted that to protect their own.

"Don't move," the man said again as Nick put his book down back on the shelf behind him.

Nick really looked at the man and he was hot, that was a definite truth. Nick really liked the man's strong sexy jawline, smooth radiant skin and the man was tall, seriously tall.

Nick had had a lot of boyfriends in the past, some Scottish, some French and some English. But they had never been this tall before, the man had to be at least 7 foot tall and he was seriously hot because of it.

And judging by the man's accent he was certainly from around London, and whilst Nick had lost his accent and Scottish dialect because it was the only way to make the English and MI5 take you seriously, Nick just knew that he had to be extremely careful.

"What lies did they tell about me?" Nick asked.

The hot man grinned a little, a very cute one at that. "They didn't lie. It is you that have lied you Scottish terrorist. You are a threat to the UK and I will not let you kill the Justice,"

It was amazing how much of an open book this MI5 hot man was. Clearly he didn't like the Scottish that much was clear from his voice, clearly he thought Nick was a terrorist and that the Justice was an innocent person which made sense because of the rigged ruling tomorrow but Nick couldn't understand why his bosses at MI5 would lie.

"Listen mate," Nick said, "I am not a terrorist. Yesterday I found a buried terrorist attack report saying that Scottish people would be bombed. I told my supervisor and she dismissed it. I go back to my office and the report is missing,"

The hot man laughed and as annoying as the laughter was, there was just something rather magical about it. And Nick really wanted to listen to it again.

"Liar. MI5 doesn't bury terrorist attack reports and I've already searched the databases and your computer for this so-called report. It isn't there,"

Nick hated the feeling of the gun pressing harder against him.

"You are a liar and a terrorist. Come with me or I will have to deal with you in front of these people," the hot man said.

Nick looked around and the three civil servants were all together now flicking through some new erotica title. They didn't even seem to be interested in what was going on here.

Nick had to protect them. If this hot man fired and he missed then those people could get hurt.

"How about I prove it to you?" Nick asked. "You said you've gone through my computers right?"

The hot man sneered and nodded.

"Then did you find a computer file by the case number of #20221109ab?"

Nick loved it how the hot man didn't look sure or anything. "And you also would have searched and gone through all my previous cases to get a sense of the man I am?"

The hot man nodded. "You are still a Scottish terrorist,"

All Nick wanted in that moment was to really shout at this sexy man that he wasn't a terrorist but he also really wanted to look at this hottie's beautiful ocean-blue eyes.

It was a silly thing to want but if Nick was about to be arrested for a crime he didn't commit then he at least wanted to remember this hottie.

"Look me in the eye and answer me this, with all

my experience, decades of service and all the English people I have protected. Do you seriously think I'm a terrorist?"

When Nick noticed the three civil servants looking at him now Nick just knew that if he didn't convince this hot man that he was innocent sooner or later then he was done for.

And so many innocent people would die in that terrorist attack.

***

Michael had to flat out give it to this Nick Blackford, not only was he extremely hot and sexy but he was also very, very good at making good points. And he actually didn't dare look into his beautiful whiskey-coloured eyes.

And Nick sadly had a great point.

Michael had spent hours reading, rereading and really trying to understand how Nick's mind worked, and besides from him being a Scottish Nationalist he didn't seem like a bad person.

In his spare time, Nick liked to donate his time to children hospitals where he would read stories to the sick children, he would also do charity fun runs and he would spend a lot of time posting on social media things in favour of Scottish Independence.

Normally Michael hated any man that wasn't local because it just made relationships really hard and Michael wasn't into gay hook-up culture, but Nick was beautiful and Michael's stomach filled with butterflies.

There was something more to this beautiful man than met the eye.

And now Michael was really thinking about it, some of the things made sense. Like it was unfair the Scots were forced into Brexit against their will, they didn't have a right to do whatever they wanted even if the UK Government was doing something stupid and they were always a slave to England.

But Michael wasn't going to let this hot sexy man interfere with his mission.

He had a job to do.

"I won't allow you to influence me," Michael said focusing on Nick's chest that was actually a mistake because his black suit made his chest seem very seductive and muscular.

Nick laughed. "Why am I influencing you? I just don't want to get arrested over some lies from MI5. And you haven't answered my question?"

Damn it. Michael really wasn't sure about Nick. He was hot and beautiful and his service record was amazing but his bosses didn't lie to him.

"Excuse gents," an elderly man said and out of instinct Michael hid the gun by his side but the elderly man wearing the long red cloak of the Supreme Court Justices kept looking at him.

Michael let instinct take over and he kissed Nick.

Michael moaned a damn slight louder than he meant to as he was shocked at how large, soft and delicious Nick's lips were.

Out of the corner of his eye, Michael watched

the Justice smile to himself and he went to over to the erotica bookshelf.

Michael broke the kiss and just looked at Nick. He looked so adorable with his big wide eyes, cute little grin and his amazing black-suited body.

"You don't think I'm a terrorist?" Nick asked.

Michael stomped his feet gently on the ground. "Damn you. I don't think anything at the moment but tell me what you were apparently going to do to the Justice if you aren't a terrorist,"

"I am not a terrorist," Nick said.

Michael shrugged like he didn't believe him but that sort of felt like a massive lie to him. Michael had hunted hundreds of terrorists on UK soil for the past twenty years and sadly Nick just didn't feel like one.

Michael tensed a little as Nick got out a very small black device that Michael knew was a phone-cloner and he turned it on.

"I was going to clone the Justice's phone and leave. That's the truth," Nick said.

Michael wasn't sure if he believed him but Michael took the cloner off Nick. "I'll make you a deal. If you agree not to run off or commit any terror offences, I will clone the Justice's phone and we will review the data together,"

Beautiful Nick didn't exactly look sure but Michael really wanted him to take the deal because it would still allow Michael to spend time with him (and he only wanted to do that to keep the criminal in sight, of course) and hopefully Michael could learn a little more about this utterly beautiful man.

"Fine," Nick said.

It took every little gram of willpower that Michael had not to jump up and down in the air. But he didn't want to look stupid and he also didn't want the Justice to be scared away.

Michael went off.

He had a phone to clone and a beautiful man to get to know a little better.

***

Nick seriously hadn't expected to basically be a prisoner in all-but-name and standing at the very beautiful fake-marble kitchen island in the middle of Michael's flat. Nick had to admit that the flat was stunning and it felt so nice to be in Michael's flat with its massive black sofas and armchairs, very modern and cosy kitchen and the very impressive wine collection.

Nick had only heard of some of the wine brands that Michael had, let alone actually seen them in real life. He might have been Scottish but Nick did love a good glass of wine.

Michael had set up his very secure laptop on the kitchen island and Nick stood behind the hot man that he was falling for more and more with each passing moment.

"I'm just sorting through the data now," Michael said.

Nick was surprised at how well Michael was taking this, Nick was fairly sure he would be dead or in handcuffs by now because Michael seemed to be the sort of intelligence officer that followed orders without thinking about them.

Nick had no problem with those sort of officers but sometimes orders and intelligence needed to be questioned because it was the right thing to do and it needed to be.

And Nick seriously hoped that the information they got from the Justice's phone would be good.

At the very least it would buy Nick a little more time to make a decision about what he needed to be and maybe, just maybe it would convince Michael that he was innocent.

But he wasn't holding his hopes up very high.

As beautiful, sexy and hot as Michael was, he was an Intelligence Officer first and foremost and Nick just had the sense that he always followed orders no matter what or if they were right.

So Nick was half-planning on how to make a good escape.

"Here," Michael said. "I think this is what you were looking for,"

Nick leant over hot Michael and got so close to him that Nick got to feel hard Michael's perfect body was and Michael pressed slightly against him.

"You shouldn't be doing that," Michael said seductively.

"You shouldn't be letting me," Nick said resting his head on Michael's shoulder.

Then Nick realised that Michael was showing

him the recent call logs and bank transfers from the Justice's banking app to a number of international accounts.

Of course there was nothing strange about that at all but considering all the transactions were to countries and accounts that were hostile to the UK that seemed just a tat weird.

"Running the accounts now," Michael said as his laptop screen changed to show a map of the world with dots flying all over the screen.

Nick was impressed that Michael's first thought had been to track the endpoint of the money and not the account name itself. That was a great idea that Nick wouldn't have thought of alone.

It was times like that Nick really loved working with other officers.

"Why go out on your own?" Michael asked.

Nick was expecting to get a lecture on protocol, rules and all the other stuff that he really didn't care about when innocent lives were at stake. But there was just something in Michael's stunning eyes that made him realise Michael was asking about *his* reasons.

Michael actually seemed to care about what *Nick* wanted and that was rare in Nick's life.

"Because I joined MI5 twenty years ago to help protect innocent people. At the time I didn't care about protecting the Union, Scotland or any single country or government. I only cared about protecting the innocent,"

Michael slowly nodded. "And now?"

Nick laughed because to him the answer was clear as day. "And now all I want in the entire world is for every single innocent person to be safe at night,"

Michael's mouth dropped.

"None of us in Scotland give two craps about nationality. I don't care if a person is Afghan, French, Albanian or any of the other nationalities around the world that the English propaganda tries to make out are evil."

Michael actually seemed lost for words.

"I only care that innocent people are safe. That is what twenty years of intelligence work has taught me," Nick said.

"Thank you," Michael said still looking shocked.

Nick shrugged. "That was nothing. It was the truth,"

Michael rubbed his forehead. "I know it was. I just wanted to hear and, I just wanted to hear something refreshing and someone remind me why I joined,"

Nick nodded because it was great to see that Michael was the great and wonderful man that he had pegged him for.

Michael's laptop beeped.

Nick just laughed hard when he looked at the laptop and saw all the money that the Justice had sent out had all returned to the UK. And eight other names popped up including three very high-up people in MI5, two Justices in the UK's Supreme Court and some other people that made Nick's stomach twist.

Nick just couldn't believe how far this corruption spread and it was flat outrageous that a Justice was involved with such criminal activity.

This is not what Nick wanted at all.

"We have to report this," Nick said. "We have to get these people arrested and the terrorists stopped,"

Michael shook his head and double-checked the Justice's messages and Nick laughed again.

He could read every single message between the Justice and his and Michael's bosses at MI5 as they all showed the Justice instructed his bosses to bury the terrorist chatter and get rid of whoever found it, if it was ever found.

"Okay," Michael said standing up and grinning. "I believe you,"

Nick threw his arms up in the air. "So only now you believe me. I have always been honest with you,"

Michael grinned like a little schoolboy at Nick. "I know but this is proof. You won't go to jail or die,"

"Why the hell do you care?" Nick asked.

Michael hugged him. "Because it means I can ask you out!"

Nick just broke the hug and just looked at Michael. Nick had been asked out before by a rather varied range of hot men but none of them had ever asked him out quite like this before.

"So we just met, you threatened me with terrorism charges and now you're asking me out,"

Nick said.

Michael hissed a little as he probably realised how weird that sounded.

"I'll think about it," Nick said. "Let's just expose this corruption,"

Nick went to grab the laptop when Michael put his hands in Nick's. "Actually you might be Scottish and you might have different ways, but these people are English targets. So we're going to treat them the English way,"

Nick just shook his head because Scotland was all about justice, peace and doing what was ethical. And if his time in England had taught him anything, it was that those rules didn't apply to the rich and powerful.

And all the 8 people identified were very rich and extremely powerful.

***

Michael was extremely glad when hot beautiful Nick had agreed to his idea about confronting their former boss. And after they had both showered (sadly not together), Michael was seriously amazed at how sexy Nick looked in a crisp white shirt, black jeans and black shoes.

It was definitely taking every single gram of willpower Michael had not to ask Nick to have sex with him right there and then.

"What do I owe this pleasure?" a woman asked wearing a very tight and ill-fitting black business dress and thick black glasses.

Michael, with sexy Nick behind him, went into a

very small but posh office with great brown walls, a glass cabinet filled with whiskey to the left and a very dusty bookshelf to the right.

"I see you got me the terrorist," she said.

Michael just smiled as he took out his laptop and placed it in front of his boss.

"Now, what is this?" she asked.

"This," Nick said failing to hide the anger in his voice but that only made him cuter. "Is proof that you were paid a lot of money by a Supreme Court Justice,"

Michael's boss nodded like this was nothing new.

"And these," Michael said, "are the messages between you and the same Justice to bury a terrorist report and frame whoever found it,"

Michael loved seeing the flash of concern dance across his boss's face.

"This is very interest but-" she said.

"But nothing," Michael said. "This is proof and we know 7 other people were paid the same amount,"

The woman got up and went over to her glass cabinet, studying it like this was her last ever drink choice.

"We know these are all extremely powerful people," Michael said, "and I have convinced Nick here to not attack you if you agree to do something most English with us,"

The woman turned and grinned at Michael. "You want to make a deal with me so I am innocent and the other 7 people and the Supreme Court Justice are found guilty,"

Michael hated hearing Nick hiss behind him. It was completely wrong that their boss was going to get away with everything but this was the only way.

"Yes," Michael said. "It would be too impossible for my liking to investigate and find evidence of all of your corruption and your corrupt friends. So you give us the evidence, they get arrested and charged and you walk,"

The woman went back over to her desk and sat perfectly straight because she knew she was in full control of the situation.

Michael leant on the desk and tried to look as scary as he possibly could. "And you drop any hate against Nick and no terror attack against the Scots,"

The woman laughed. "Oh darling Michael, his punishment will come tomorrow and hell, all of Scotland will be punished tomorrow so my hate is meaningless,"

Michael really didn't want to know what she meant by that.

"I agree to your terms and I will get the arrest warrants for everyone and the evidence into MI5 custody, anomalously of course, by the end of the day. You have my word and I promise you both I will not come after you for this,"

Michael just shook his head. "Only because you'll get a promotion or two out of this,"

The woman grinned again as she left her office and Michael just hoped that she would stick to her word but as Nick had explained plenty of times over on the way here, when it came to the rich and powerful they only kept their word when they got even richer.

Nick came up behind Michael and hugged him. "You didn't have to do that. There were other ways,"

Michael turned around and smiled at the beautiful man and his lips that were only a few centimetres away.

"Maybe," Michael said, "but sometimes you need to make deals with the devil. The UK functions on corrupt deal after deal. If we arrested every corrupt person in the UK then there wouldn't be a government left,"

Nick weakly smiled. "I know and that's what my country wants to change,"

Michael laughed at himself because if Nick had said that a few hours ago he might have gotten defensive and moaned at Nick for being silly but now, but now he actually wanted to hear more and just understand Nick a little more.

Definitely not for political reasons because Michael doubted he would ever believe in the same things as Nick, but because Nick was a beautiful, clever man that had really grown on him the past few hours.

And after twenty years of intelligence work, Michael would have liked to believe he was great at knowing what people were like, the sort of person they were and if he could trust them with his life.

Michael wouldn't trust a single person at MI5 but he would trust Nick. The beautiful, hot, clever man that he was seriously falling for.

And a very beautiful man that Michael didn't want to say goodbye to just yet.

"Let me buy you a drink," Michael said.

***

Nick never ever would have imagined last night being quite as magical, perfect and spellbinding as it had been when Michael had taken him out for the most wonderful dinner he had ever had. They went for French food at a local posh restaurant, where they had laughed, joked and had amazing fun.

Then they had gone to some dance clubs and kissed a little and really had some fun last night.

Nick stood in front of a large glass window in Michael's bedroom with hot sexy Michael still in bed empty behind him. Nick had to admit that Michael had a sensational flat and a very nice bedroom with black silk bedsheets, very supportive pillows and a built-in wardrobe.

The morning air was crisp, cold and cosy. Nick was really looking forward to when Michael woke up because Nick wouldn't mind a round two after last night and it would just be great to chat more.

In his past relationships Nick had never really been one for talking because he had never been able to talk about work, his missions and his kills before, but this time was different.

All last night and when they been feeling

together, Nick had had the strangest feeling in the world and Nick was only realising now what it was. It was the feeling that being with Michael was very natural to him.

When they were at dinner, the dance club and even in bed, there had never been an awkward silence, a moment of boredom and everything just went so smoothly. Nick had never had that with a man before, there had always been strange moments that killed the mood because conversations stopped or something.

With Michael that never happened.

Nick looked at Michael as he started stirring, they both blew each other a kiss and then Michael checked his phone a little. Nick was hoping he would confirm that their boss did do as she said she would, because Nick had only checked the Supreme Court's ruling on the independence case. Which of course they rejected, the precious Union wasn't going to let Scotland go without a fight.

But Scotland would be free one day that was a promise.

"She did it," Michael said as he got up in only his pink boxers that somehow managed to make him look even hotter.

Nick kissed him and Michael just looked into his eyes with an expression that wasn't quite sad or happy, it was something in-between.

"What?" Nick asked.

Michael kissed Nick again. "I don't know. I like you. I like you a lot but is this going to work? We don't agree with politics, we don't agree on backroom deals and we don't agree on-"

Nick just kissed him. "I believe in this. I have never felt as good with a man as I have with you. I want to see exactly where this relationship goes because I know it will go far,"

Both men smiled like teenage boys at each other and Nick kissed Michael again and again. Then Nick pushed Michael away gently when he started getting a little too excited.

"But if you really doubt any of this relationship then I'll know. We both have to go to work today and tackle a new case," Nick said.

Michael nodded.

"So I'm going to take a shower and if you want this relationship then join me. If you don't, go to work and I'll know what I mean to you," Nick said.

As soon as Nick said the words he wanted to take it all back because he didn't want to give Michael an excuse not to come with him. He wanted, needed a relationship with Michael more than anything else in the world.

Nick would have happily given up being an intelligence officer if it meant spending another day with Michael.

That was exactly how much he cared about Michael.

"Okay," Michael said weakly smiling.

Nick went off to the shower and closed the shower door, stripped down and started having a shower. He really wanted Michael to join him and he seriously wanted their relationship to last forever but he knew there was a minor chance that it wouldn't happen.

Moments later the shower door opened and Nick felt two very strong manly arms wrap around him and beautiful lips started kissing his back.

And Nick immediately knew that their relationship was going to be fine, would probably last forever and Michael was just as into Nick as he was into him.

Nick and Michael were late to work after a quick round two. And that was perfectly fine with both of them because they would both always love, protect and treasure each other for the rest of their lives.

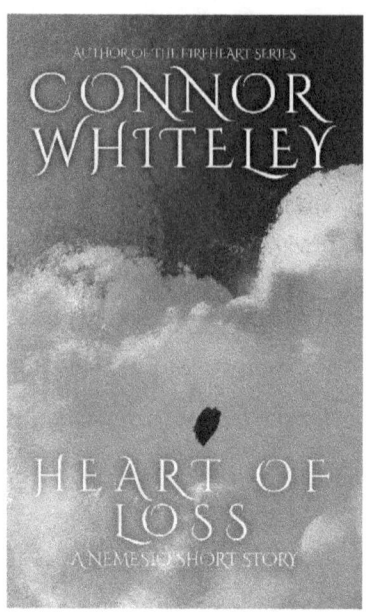

GET YOUR FREE AND EXCLUSIVE SHORT STORY NOW! LEARN ABOUT NEMESIO'S PAST!

https://www.subscribepage.com/fireheart

Keep up to date with exclusive deals on Connor Whiteley's Books, as well as the latest news about new releases and so much more!

Sign up for the Grab a Book and Chill Monthly newsletter, and you'll get one **FREE** ebook just for signing up: Agents of The Emperor Collection.

Sign Up Now!

https://dl.bookfunnel.com/f4p5xkprbk

About the author:

Connor Whiteley is the author of over 60 books in the sci-fi fantasy, nonfiction psychology and books for writer's genre and he is a Human Branding Speaker and Consultant.

He is a passionate warhammer 40,000 reader, psychology student and author.

Who narrates his own audiobooks and he hosts The Psychology World Podcast.

All whilst studying Psychology at the University of Kent, England.

Also, he was a former Explorer Scout where he gave a speech to the Maltese President in August 2018 and he attended Prince Charles' 70th Birthday Party at Buckingham Palace in May 2018.

Plus, he is a self-confessed coffee lover!

OTHER SHORT STORIES BY CONNOR WHITELEY

Mystery Short Stories:
Protecting The Woman She Hated
Finding A Royal Friend
Our Woman In Paris
Corrupt Driving
A Prime Assassination
Jubilee Thief
Jubilee, Terror, Celebrations
Negative Jubilation
Ghostly Jubilation
Killing For Womenkind
A Snowy Death
Miracle Of Death
A Spy In Rome
The 12:30 To St Pancreas
A Country In Trouble
A Smokey Way To Go
A Spicy Way To GO
A Marketing Way To Go
A Missing Way To Go
A Showering Way To Go
Poison In The Candy Cane
Christmas Innocence
You Better Watch Out
Christmas Theft
Trouble In Christmas
Smell of The Lake
Problem In A Car

ROMANCE SPIES COLLECTION VOLUME 2

Theft, Past and Team
Embezzler In The Room
A Strange Way To Go
A Horrible Way To Go
Ann Awful Way To Go
An Old Way To Go
A Fishy Way To Go
A Pointy Way To Go
A High Way To Go
A Fiery Way To Go
A Glassy Way To Go
A Chocolatey Way To Go
Kendra Detective Mystery Collection Volume 1
Kendra Detective Mystery Collection Volume 2
Stealing A Chance At Freedom
Glassblowing and Death
Theft of Independence
Cookie Thief
Marble Thief
Book Thief
Art Thief
Mated At The Morgue
The Big Five Whoopee Moments
Stealing An Election
Mystery Short Story Collection Volume 1
Mystery Short Story Collection Volume 2
Criminal Performance
Candy Detectives
Key To Birth In The Past

<u>Science Fiction Short Stories:</u>
Temptation
Superhuman Autospy
Blood In The Redwater
All Is Dust
Vigil
Emperor Forgive Us
Their Brave New World
Gummy Bear Detective
The Candy Detective
What Candies Fear
The Blurred Image
Shattered Legions
The First Rememberer
Life of A Rememberer
System of Wonder
Lifesaver
Remarkable Way She Died
The Interrogation of Annabella Stormic
Blade of The Emperor
Arbiter's Truth
Computation of Battle
Old One's Wrath
Puppets and Masters
Ship of Plague
Interrogation
Edge of Failure
One Way Choice
Acceptable Losses
Balance of Power

ROMANCE SPIES COLLECTION VOLUME 2

Good Idea At The Time
Escape Plan
Escape In The Hesitation
Inspiration In Need
Singing Warriors
Knowledge is Power
Killer of Polluters
Climate of Death
The Family Mailing Affair
Defining Criminality
The Martian Affair
A Cheating Affair
The Little Café Affair
Mountain of Death
Prisoner's Fight
Claws of Death
Bitter Air
Honey Hunt
Blade On A Train
<u>Fantasy Short Stories:</u>
City of Snow
City of Light
City of Vengeance
Dragons, Goats and Kingdom
Smog The Pathetic Dragon
Don't Go In The Shed
The Tomato Saver
The Remarkable Way She Died
The Bloodied Rose
Asmodia's Wrath

Heart of A Killer
Emissary of Blood
Dragon Coins
Dragon Tea
Dragon Rider
Sacrifice of the Soul
Heart of The Flesheater
Heart of The Regent
Heart of The Standing
Feline of The Lost
Heart of The Story
City of Fire
Awaiting Death

Other books by Connor Whiteley:
Bettie English Private Eye Series
A Very Private Woman
The Russian Case
A Very Urgent Matter
A Case Most Personal
Trains, Scots and Private Eyes
The Federation Protects

Lord of War Origin Trilogy:
Not Scared Of The Dark
Madness
Burn It All

The Fireheart Fantasy Series
Heart of Fire
Heart of Lies
Heart of Prophecy
Heart of Bones
Heart of Fate

City of Assassins (Urban Fantasy)
City of Death
City of Marytrs
City of Pleasure
City of Power

Agents of The Emperor
Return of The Ancient Ones
Vigilance
Angels of Fire
Kingmaker
The Eight
The Lost Generation
Lord Of War Trilogy (Agents of The Emperor)
Not Scared Of The Dark
Madness
Burn It All Down

The Garro Series- Fantasy/Sci-fi
GARRO: GALAXY'S END
GARRO: RISE OF THE ORDER
GARRO: END TIMES
GARRO: SHORT STORIES

GARRO: COLLECTION
GARRO: HERESY
GARRO: FAITHLESS
GARRO: DESTROYER OF WORLDS
GARRO: COLLECTIONS BOOK 4-6
GARRO: MISTRESS OF BLOOD
GARRO: BEACON OF HOPE
GARRO: END OF DAYS

Winter Series- Fantasy Trilogy Books
WINTER'S COMING
WINTER'S HUNT
WINTER'S REVENGE
WINTER'S DISSENSION

Miscellaneous:
RETURN
FREEDOM
SALVATION
Reflection of Mount Flame
The Masked One
The Great Deer

Gay Romance Novellas
Breaking, Nursing, Repairing A Broken Heart
Jacob And Daniel
Fallen For A Lie
His Heartstopper
Spying And Weddings

www.ingramcontent.com/pod-product-compliance
Lightning Source LLC
LaVergne TN
LVHW012110070526
838202LV00056B/5686